Allies

Novella 5

Habitual Humanity

Series

J. M. Tompkins

Copyright ©2020 by Creativity Untamed, LLC

ISBN: 9798577008147

Cover Illustration by Rebecacovers

Cover Photos by Boscorelli and Zabelin

Typography & formatting by Typographer Creativity Untamed, LLC

Editing services provided by Darcy Werkman (AKA The Bearded Book Editor)

All rights reserved. No part of this publication may be reproduced, stored in a retrieval system, or transmitted in any form or by any means, electronic, mechanical, recording or otherwise, without the prior written permission of the copyright holder.

This is a work of fiction. Names, characters, businesses, places, events, and incidents are either the products of the author's imagination or used in a fictitious manner. Any resemblance to actual persons, living or dead, or actual events is purely coincidental.

For my son,

I love you until the ends of Earth and beyond.

CONTENTS

ACKNOWLEDGEMENTS 0

THURSDAY | JUNE 8, 2073 0

FRIDAY | JUNE 9, 2073 4

FRIDAY | JUNE 9, 2073 8

FRIDAY | JUNE 9, 2073 14

FRIDAY | JUNE 9, 2073 22

FRIDAY | JUNE 9, 2073 26

MONDAY | JUNE 12, 2073 29

THURSDAY | JUNE 15, 2073 33

SATURDAY | JUNE 17, 2073 39

SATURDAY | JUNE 17, 2073 43

SATURDAY | JUNE 17, 2073 46

SATURDAY | JUNE 17, 2073 51

SATURDAY | JUNE 17, 2073 54

SUNDAY | JUNE 18, 2073 58

SUNDAY | JUNE 18, 2073 63

SUNDAY | JUNE 18, 2073 66

MONDAY | JUNE 19, 2073 73

MONDAY | JUNE 19, 2073..79

TUESDAY | JUNE 20, 2073 81

TUESDAY | JUNE 20, 2073 84

TUESDAY | JUNE 20, 2073 87

THURSDAY | JUNE 22, 2073 91

FRIDAY | JUNE 23, 2073 94

FRIDAY | JUNE 23, 2073 97

FRIDAY | JUNE 23, 2073 101

FRIDAY | JUNE 23, 2073 104

SATURDAY | JUNE 24, 2073..108

SATURDAY | JUNE 24, 2073..113

TUESDAY | JUNE 27, 2073 116

ACKNOWLEDGEMENTS..119

ABOUT THE AUTHOR 120

ACKNOWLEDGEMENTS

Allies exists because of a supportive and loving group of people I like to refer to as Team 2020. I'm so grateful to Brad Tompkins, Meg M. Robinson, Justin Joseph, Jennifer Drummand, Kitty Wynn Gavel, Elaine Tompkins, Darcy Werkman (AKA The Bearded Book Editor), RebecaCovers, Chris Negron, and Toni Bellon. And to both of my writing groups, you are the first eyes on every project. Thank you.

THURSDAY | JUNE 8, 2073

AUGUST PAXTON

Laurel, Montana had always been a quiet place. Never too much traffic or excitement. Laws were rarely broken other than speed limits and petty shoplifting by kids daring each other to test the limits. It had never hit the radar for any major businesses and, therefore, had never been considered for a live-work community.

Once those live-work communities began incorporating the Utopias—the gigantic vertical factories where much of the food and raw materials could be grown from biological 3-D printers—the economy of the small town was destroyed, and Laurel, like many others, was left destitute. Without support coming from the government, the only choice was to start a mini economy. That meant that they had to do what they could to survive, and that was working together.

The government didn't try to stop them, per se, but when some of the starving and desperate outsiders started protesting and rioting, martial law was put into effect. Things got even harder for the small town then, at least until the military shrunk to the point that it could no longer enforce

HABITUAL HUMANITY

the law outside of the live-work communities. That's when the split happened. Those in the live-work communities thrived, by their own standards at least, and outsiders made their own communities without the law to get in their way.

Now, Laurel was a thriving community of outsiders. Each neighbor helped one another, for the most part anyway, and they had what they needed to get by. There were no judgments of fashion or career; it was a community of people who lived, simple as that.

Located on the outskirts of Laurel, the Paxton ranch was a quiet place. When August Paxton was on his way home after a long day in the field, he stopped short when he saw a strange vehicle parked sideways in his driveway and his front door wide open. He stood there a moment, staring at the gaping open threshold in disbelief. Had the military found him? It couldn't be; they wouldn't have shown up in a beat-up gray Honda with expired non-military license plates after all this time. It could be someone that needed help, or it could be some asshole with no respect for anyone whatsoever.

When he climbed the porch steps, he remembered that they had creaked for years, and it'd never occurred to him to fix them. So, when he climbed the steps, he put his foot on the far right of the first step. It was silent. He continued to the next step, still careful of where he placed his foot. Then he heard a woman yelling indecipherable words from inside.

Abandoning all caution, he sprinted to the front door and hit the secret spot on the craftsman-style pediment. The panel popped open and a shotgun fell into his hands. He took two steps and pointed the barrel into the living room. It was empty, and everything was just as he'd left it. He took a few more steps, past the stairs that hugged the east side of the house, and pointed his gun into the kitchen.

"August!" The voice carried from upstairs.

August spun, rushed back toward the stairs, and bolted up toward the second story.

"August!"

HABITUAL HUMANITY

"Audrey?" he yelled in disbelief. There was no way it could be her.

"August!"

The familiar voice that had yelled his name more times than he could count confirmed it was, beyond a doubt, his sister. She was supposed to be taking care of their sick parents in Sacramento. How could she be here?

Audrey came limping out of his room, the same place where their parents had always slept until they had no choice but to go to California with her.

Audrey stopped short when she saw the gun pointed in her direction. She was covered in dirt, her clothes were torn, and her arms and face were a greenish-yellow of old bruises. August looked into his sister's eyes, which were normally kind and calm, and saw panic in them. It was like looking into Darius' eyes after the events that took place in the Wastebasket—wide-eyed, constantly searching for danger even when it wasn't there. The dreams still haunted him four years later, but August couldn't think about that now.

"Audrey?" August asked in a soft tone as he leaned down to place the shotgun on the floor. He then reached out to her and put both of his hands on her shoulders. "What's going on?"

Tears streamed down her face as she began to sob.

He wrapped her in his arms. The smell was horrific, a combination of dirt, blood, and rancid body odor. He did his best not to recoil. "Shhhh, what happened?"

"It was horrible," she said, her voice cracking as she spoke between sobs.

Where were their sick parents? What about her husband, Patrick?

She fell to her knees, thudding as she hit the hardwood floor. On Audrey's prom night, she'd been right here, on this very landing, crying from being stood up and heartbroken on one of the most important events of high school. Their mother hadn't been able to console her, but August was the one that finally got her to talk, and he knew he could do it again. Just as he did then, he sat on the floor next to her, keeping his arms wrapped around her, and asked again in a soft voice for her to tell him what happened.

"They . . ." She sobbed, choking on the memory. August would give her all the time she needed. After a moment she tried again. "Outsiders were burning the city from the perimeter in. The mayor directed everyone to return home and wait while they launched a counterattack. But I couldn't get home; transportation had been halted. I couldn't call anyone because the cell towers were knocked out. I had to walk, and by the time I got home, the building was on fire. The whole—" She started to sob again.

August didn't urge her to continue. He knew she lived on the twelfth floor of an apartment building, and since their parents were bedridden, living with her so they could get free medical treatment available only to citizens, that meant they'd been inside. There was just one thing left to ask.

"Where's Patrick?"

"I had hoped he was here!" she wailed. "I didn't know where else to go. I had to run out of Sacramento, and there was so much violence. I was terrified. I just kept going. I made it to Nevada, and that's when I stole that car. I didn't know what else to do."

FRIDAY | JUNE 9, 2073

DARIUS JONES

Darius took his plate to the kitchen to handwash it along with the pan, spatula, and fork. When he was done, he turned and wiped down the stove. He checked his watch. He had five minutes until he needed to leave. The routine was off; he didn't know what to do with himself. The silence turned into a pulsating noise in his head. He took his glasses off and rubbed his nose.

When Gia lived next door, he could hear her television or her bath running. Sometimes, he could even hear her lovemaking with Joel. That part he preferred to do without, but even that was at least the sound of other humans. Once she had learned of her pregnancy, her and Joel had married and moved into a house close to the base to raise Barry, their son. That had left Darius totally alone in the apartment building. It had four units, and yet his was the only one occupied. Four units, each with at least five rooms, all but one of which were void of life.

Taylor had left as soon as her contract was done, not being able to quite stomach the demands and secrets. There was still Mollie and Hector—the dynamic duo, as Hector liked to dub them. They lived in the adjacent building, but their regular beer and wings affair wasn't really Darius' cup of tea. That left Darius alone. Alone with the black hole of which the only things that escaped were his thoughts and worries. Alone with his books that could only keep the depression at bay for an hour at most. And lately, alone with a bottle of wine he'd start but never finish. He'd often end up looking at the bottle as though it were an acquaintance he didn't really like. Deciding that drinking alone wouldn't end well, he'd then pour over half of the bottle down the drain. The habit had somehow become a part of his routine— heading on a nice walk after work, meandering down the aisles of the liquor store, and finally, more from the guilt of looking and not buying, purchasing an award-winning bottle.

His daily routine also consistently began with an early morning call with August. He insisted they still had something. And Darius did love August, more than he ever imagined he'd love anyone. His vision of himself was that he'd marry his work, and so, their connection had taken him by surprise. But time had passed, and the question about what their future could possibly be had become the unspoken threat to their relationship. Maybe he was in love with the idea of August, or the idea of a relationship, if that's what they truly had.

Sometimes Darius' physical needs overcame his love for August. He no longer lived under the restriction of not being able to leave the base now that the secret project of military dupes was known across the world. And he had, on more than one occasion, sought out someone with similar needs. None of them had brought up the emotions like August did. None of them became more than a one-night deal.

He closed his eyes tightly, still standing in the kitchen. He didn't want to remember cheating on August, or wonder if August had done the same. It had been four years.

The dread began to take him, forcing him to envision August with another man and shattering his heart. It was the black hole swallowing him again. He had to be busy. Besides, it was time for work, not pity or regret. Darius checked his watch. It was time. He put his glasses on and grabbed his briefcase. Stick to the routine and everything will be fine—get up, shower, make eggs, and work.

He stepped out the front door, and the bolt slid into place as he walked away. After taking a few steps, he stopped to wait for Hector and Mollie to join him. They were sleepy as usual from staying up too late, and Hector held his huge coffee mug up toward Darius in a form of hello. Routines were good.

"Good morning," Darius said.

"Morn'," Hector replied his in usual moody morning tone.

"Hello, Darius," Mollie said in her normal chipper voice. "I saw this crazy documentary last night!"

Darius smiled and nodded, but Hector groaned, "Without me?"

"You went to bed early!"

"*Darius* goes to bed early. And I didn't go to bed that late! Besides, I was tired."

"You're always tired. So anyway, it was about this woman that was murdered."

"Don't tell us the ending," Hector barked.

"Listen," Mollie insisted. "She was this teacher at this school . . ." Mollie rattled on, and just as she did every time, she told them who the killer was.

"No, Mollie! I told you not to tell us!" Hector groaned.

"Darius doesn't mind!"

"Of course Darius doesn't mind. I don't think he's seen a movie or show since . . . *ever*!"

"I have watched television. I just do not watch as much as you," Darius replied.

"Well, great. You two can start walking to work together without me."

"You say that every morning," Mollie replied.

They arrived at their building and stopped to scan each of their eyes for entry. The military AI program, Alaine, greeted

HABITUAL HUMANITY

each of them warmly. That brought an end to the daily routine.

Inside, all the glass walls, which were usually set to privacy mode that displayed a dense fog, were displaying identical maps of the United States. Several locations had yellow dots—New York, Atlanta, Bentonville, Philadelphia, and Toledo, to name a few. Those were live-work communities. Then there were other areas highlighted in red. He didn't recognize the locations until he saw Laurel, Montana. Then he knew that those were the off-the-grid communities. He also noted that Sacramento was highlighted in red. In addition to the abnormal setting of the walls, General Maxwell stood in the middle of their lab next to Gia, who was hugging a trash can and looking pale and terrified.

FRIDAY | JUNE 9, 2073

GIA MORENO

General Maxwell was the last person Gia wanted to see when she came to work. Seeing a rather large man standing in the middle of the examination room made her jump, surprising her that someone was there at seven fifteen in the morning. The general was distracted by his tablet and didn't seem to notice her surprise. With the walls set to private and the general taking up so much space, the room seemed to shrink in on her.

"Good morning, General." She kept her voice even.

"Morning, ma'am." He was still the one person she hadn't been able to break from that habit no matter how many times she'd requested he not call her ma'am. "Is this your usual time to get here?"

"I'm an early riser, and I like to knock out correspondences before the day gets started. Alaine, please set the walls to open."

Instantly the glass walls changed from solid, for privacy in the examination rooms, to clear, making the examination area one giant room. Gia felt relief and was able to breathe a little easier.

"Alaine, presentation mode, please," the general commanded, his concentration never leaving his tablet. The walls switched to show the maps.

Feeling her chest tighten, Gia took a slow, deep inhale as she approached the coffee maker and began to fill the carafe with water. With the coffee brewing, she turned her attention to the maps and noticed Sacramento's red dot. "Have there been more attacks?" she asked.

"Yes, the outsiders have taken over Sacramento by attacking the largest buildings on the edge of the community and burning them down one by one," he responded gruffly. He looked up from his tablet at her. "We'll get it back. We're sending in more enforcements now. But our intelligence says there are about to be more attacks on other cities."

She understood the pressure on him to make the communities safe. She'd done some light calculations and realized that, though their dupe army was large, the outsiders could be accumulating in impressive numbers. The multitude of red dots on the map alone were staggering.

Part of her wanted the outsiders to win. When the exact moment was that she'd become an outsider at heart, she had no idea. Possibly when Darius told them what Blake and Lucky had done in the Wastebasket. Or after the executions of dupes that were too damaged to fight. Or maybe it was the size of the dupe graveyard beyond the east edge of the base. Perhaps she'd become an outsider when she'd learned of the cleansing initiative. She wasn't sure, but the cleansing was when she understood why the Warrens had gone AWOL.

Simultaneously, Gia was terrified of the outsiders. Being a citizen meant that she was their enemy. And if she ever went AWOL to become an outsider, the military would hunt her down, and then what would happen to her son and husband? The military didn't waste any time hunting down the Warrens and executing them. For the sake of her family, going AWOL wasn't an option. Torn, Gia both hoped that they'd succeed and that they'd fail. The biggest hope, and the only thing that mattered, was that her son, Barry, would live to see a safe and just world.

"When do the others usually get here?" the general asked.

He'd taken her out of her thoughts. She looked down at her watch and ignored the blinking that indicated her heart rate and blood pressure were elevated. "They'll get here soon. It's only seven thirty, and they don't have to be here until eight."

"It's better to get things accomplished, don't you think?" he said sharply.

Gia realized that he must have some pressing news if he was anxious to get started. "I can text them and let them know something urgent has come up."

"No, don't alarm anyone," the general grunted. He walked away from her and toward the coffee pot. "Thank you for the coffee. It smells delicious."

"You're welcome, General." Gia turned back toward her tablet and attempted to focus on her e-mails, or at least to *look* like she was focused on her e-mails. Then it occurred to her that if she wanted more information, maybe she should just ask.

"General? How big is the outsider army?"

He turned quickly toward her. His eyes fell briefly to the floor and he turned back around again. He put two sugars and one creamer in his cup, and then, as he pulled the pot from the maker, he glanced over at her. "We're thinking over a hundred thousand. We're working on a program that will use drones to count bodies and analyze formations. We're estimating their army size by formation." Having filled his cup, he returned the pot and walked over to her.

"Because societies tend to spread out or up, but a group of people training for war takes on a different pattern," Gia responded.

The general pulled up a stool across from her and sat down, sipping his coffee with a loud *slurp*. "You got it. We're limited by the ability to have a human analyze the information, in my opinion. Sure, the drones are programmed and armed with AI, but we don't know what they don't know to tell us. Plus, we may not have found all their bases. They may not be working together, but they could be. It's hard for us to know how large or coordinated they are or what we're missing."

"I know our military has shrunk with the state of the global economy, but we're still bigger than the outsider army." She purposefully said it as a statement and not as a question so as not to insult him.

The general smiled. He actually smiled. "Yeah, we are. But—" he raised his eyebrows and leaned forward "—never underestimate the power of strategy."

Gia was surprised. She'd just assumed that the outsiders would be taken for granted as dumb people. And she, perhaps, was guilty of that very thing at times. "You think they could actually defeat the U.S. military?"

The general leaned back against the desk behind him. "Never underestimate your opponent."

That's for sure. She didn't flinch at the statement. Instead, she sat there as though their conversation was nothing more than that of a sport or food. After she'd had Barry, she had to release the excitable and energetic girl she'd been. She did, after all, have ten non-biological children that she'd programmed to fight back against the system. But then she'd become a real mother, and everything changed. Though she constantly wondered what her non-biological children were up to, sometimes she imagined her program had failed and they weren't strategizing against the United States. But what if she was wrong, and they were doing just as she'd planned? Would they do something rash? If they did, would the military realize it was her that was behind it all? And then what would happen to Barry? Her fear for her son ran so deep she often didn't sleep.

So far, her ten had received no special recognition. They'd simply been shuffled into the fold, and everyone had been happy that her findings for speeding up the cloning process and Mama's Recipe had worked as expected. But still, deep dark secrets festered and ate upon their vessel. There was rarely a moment she felt safe—as though special operatives were constantly hiding outside her door to put a bullet in her head.

The general was staring at Gia like there was something else he may, or may not, tell her. He sipped his coffee and paused. Then he turned, placing the cup down on the desk, and gave his attention back to Gia.

"There's something else. Right now, it's confidential. I'm not planning on sharing it with your team, but it's so big that we'll have no choice but to go public sooner rather than later."

She showed no reaction other than a soft nod. "You have my confidence."

He nodded in response. "We have trouble from the inside, too. A group. We don't know how big, or how many. But they've hacked into the databases of the government, X-Over, Green Mart, and I.T. And they've released a virus that's changing the data."

Gia tilted her head to the side. It'd been over a decade since a hack was able to do any real damage. Not that people stopped trying—they were always trying—but their entire way of life was so intricately woven in data that it was imperative to keep it safe. If anything happened to their information, then society, as they knew it, would collapse.

She asked, "How bad is it?"

"It's bad. It's this slow, stealthy little bug they created. It's changing a few numbers a day, one at a time. I don't mean 5,622 to 9,729. I mean it's changing one single digit at a time, and only a few a day. We found it last month. We have no idea who did it or how long it's been there. Could have been there for a week or it could have been doing it for years."

"What data did it change? Financial?" Usually hackers went for the finances along with some slogan about following the money.

"Specifically, consumer data. It's an obvious attack

HABITUAL HUMANITY

against the citizen code."

A sinking feeling took over her stomach. She was short of breath. And that wasn't like her—she never lost her reserve.

The general nodded at her response and leaned back against the desk again. "That was the way I reacted, too. Soon, we're going to have to freeze the citizen scores. That's far from ideal, but we have no other option until we begin to figure out what's been compromised."

"So, the people who have low scores . . ."

"Will remain with shitty scores and no hope of improvement until we figure it out."

The sinking feeling continued. She felt nauseous. Before she had time to prepare, she realized she was going to lose her stomach. Her mouth quickly filled with saliva, and she reached for the trash can, vomiting her breakfast and coffee into it.

"My feelings exactly," the general said.

But the thing was, no matter how scared or nervous she got, she never threw up. The only time she'd ever thrown up was . . . then a realization hit her. And with it, terror. She leaned over the trash and lost her stomach again.

The general was standing next to her and handed her a wet paper towel. She hadn't even realized he'd gotten anything for her.

"Are you that sensitive to bad news? Or do you have other news?"

His voice wasn't unkind. He didn't sound like an authority figure as he asked it. She was shocked to experience this softer side of him.

"I don't know," she answered honestly. What else could she say? If she was pregnant, she wouldn't be able to keep that a secret forever, though she'd much rather have this moment with Joel, her husband, than the general.

And then, Darius, Mollie, and Hector entered the office.

FRIDAY | JUNE 9, 2073

STELLA HOPKINS

When someone in Fines Creek had an emergency, no beepers went off, no alarms sounded. Stella had learned quickly to listen for the sound of a speeding truck or a breathless neighbor. Those were the sounds that always preceded "There's been an accident!" or "Something's wrong!" She'd gotten so attuned to the sounds that she usually greeted the patient in the parking lot, much to their surprise.

That's what happened right when she was finishing with her last patient. A truck came barreling up the drive, crunching the gravel and sliding to a stop in front of the practice. Stella smiled at her current patient who'd made an appointment to talk about fertility. Stella didn't specialize in fertility, but she was one of only two doctors the town had. Squeezing the patient's hand, she said, "Sounds like I'm needed. Keep tracking your ovulation and give it another month. We'll check your hormone levels as discussed and see if we find anything that might be hindering the egg from attaching."

Exiting the room and closing the door for the patient's

privacy, she glanced quickly out the window. It was Chris' truck, from the other side of town. He rarely came this way. And he didn't seem to particularly like listening to ideas from a woman, or from someone who was black, or perhaps it was because she was a black woman. But these were the leveling times when someone who didn't like you, really needed you. For Chris to come to her, she knew it had to be bad.

"Hurry!" he called out to her while running to the other side of his truck as she exited the door.

Stella, already reaching for the wheelchair she kept near the front entrance, could recognize the panic mode. Chris was stumbling over his feet and running his fingers through his hair, and the edge to his tone suggested he was trying not to cry. She pushed the chair across the rocky walkway. She needed a cement truck to pave her a nice wheelchair ramp, but such things were luxuries away from the live-work communities. Those were the types of things she missed.

Chris was already pulling his wife out of the passenger seat. She clutched at her left arm and her head bobbed as Stella helped Chris maneuver her into the wheelchair. A heart attack, Stella was sure, and she estimated that it had taken Chris at least thirty minutes to drive here.

Once they were inside, Stella had her nurse, Jevan—who'd proven his talent with medical science—take her vitals while she prepared the surgery room. As soon they transferred her onto the tiny metal table, she flatlined. Stella immediately began CPR, but after ten minutes, it was clear that it was too late; Chris' wife died on the table.

When Stella announced the time of death, Jevan's shoulders slumped and he closed his eyes. He looked broken. It was his first loss, and the first is always the hardest, although it is never easy for anyone, no matter how many times it happened. As if losing a patient wasn't hard enough for Stella, seeing her son like that was harder.

Usually, she and Jevan went home together, but today, she told him to catch a ride with his dad, Deon, who always came by to see them right after five. Jevan would need to focus on letting this one go. He was sensitive and tended to carry things with him for a while, so she knew this would affect him deeply.

Back as a citizen, she'd have pulled the new team member aside, giving him a pep talk about how the first loss on the table was the hardest and how she'd be there for him. She'd have told him that the way to handle it is by turning his attention to the next patient, to keep going. But Jevan wasn't a new team member, he was her son. He also wasn't a new grad from medical school; by all civilization's means of measurement, he was a high schooler—a high schooler dealing with watching his first patient die. Suddenly, she regretted ever allowing him to join her at the practice.

She drove home alone in a somber mood. It was times like these she missed California the most—she missed being able to meet Naomi somewhere for dinner. They usually went for sushi, and how Stella missed sushi. Over a glass of wine or sake, they'd talk all the negative out of their life and reassure each other that they were trying their best.

The trouble was that the person who died today wasn't someone she'd never met. She wasn't someone that entered into a large hospital and by a random series of coincidences that spanned both chance and time was handed Stella as her doctor. Stella would see Chris again—when they traded supplies or at community meetings—and each time she'd empathize with the pain he felt. She wouldn't be able to help but picture him sitting alone at the dinner table each night and waking up alone in bed each morning. Some people thought that working as a doctor in a small town was ideal, but the truth is that it was harder. Much, much harder.

When she finally made it to her house, it wasn't strange that all the lights were off or that Deon's truck wasn't there. She'd told Deon to help Jevan distract himself, to fill his evening with positive things to remember that life is good, even when it was crushing. But, she wondered, did they eat? It was pretty late to start cooking, but there were worse things in the world than eating dinner late, like dying on the surgery table.

She slid out of her car, entered the house, and headed straight for the kitchen, where Deon would have left a note. Sure enough, there was a piece of paper with horrid, scribbled handwriting. Deon's handwriting was bad enough when he tried to be neat, so she could tell this was written in a big hurry, which sent a panic through her soul. "Gone to Jake's. Come right away."

What else could happen today? Wasn't it already bad enough? She put the note back down on the counter and took a deep breath. She reminded herself that fate didn't know when enough was enough. Just because something had already happened didn't mean nothing else would, as fate didn't know the difference between good and bad. The only control she had was to persevere no matter what. She spun around and headed right back toward the car. This time, she connected her old cell and played Otis Redding on her drive.

She smiled as *Sitting on the Dock of the Bay* bellowed out of the cheap speakers, and before *Try a Little Tenderness* finished, she was pulling up to Jake and Naomi's house. Jake and Deon had built this beautiful little hideaway into the mountain themselves, and Stella had to admit that they'd done a good job. She was proud of her husband for doing so much for others and for making this community a wonderful place. With him by her side, she could do anything.

As she got out of her car, she noticed an SUV with military tags parked beside Jake's truck. A quick panic ripped through her that the military needed them back. She had to remind herself that they weren't citizens anymore, so that couldn't happen, even though she knew that if the government needed them, a simple citizen score that could easily be manipulated by a few keystrokes wouldn't stop them. In fact, she genuinely believed nothing could stop the military from gaining whatever they wanted, but now wasn't the time to consider the corruption of government and politics.

HABITUAL HUMANITY

She didn't even bother knocking on the front door—not the one on her best friend's house anyway. They didn't bother knocking on her door either. Family didn't have to knock.

The kitchen was in the back of the house, but she didn't go that way just yet. She diverted down the hall to Sean's bedroom where, more than likely, the boys would be playing the same video games they'd mastered a long time ago. They could still challenge one another, and it was something to do.

"Ha, there's no way you can get a higher score than me," Sean was saying when she stuck her head into the room.

"You just watch," Jevan replied, leaning over as he pressed the buttons on the controller frantically. Jevan was smiling, and that was all that Stella needed to see right now.

She pulled away without disturbing the boys and headed down the hall toward the kitchen where the muffled voices barely reached her. Usually, Naomi, Jake, and Deon were laughing, and loud. The low voices meant they were talking about something so serious they didn't want the boys to know.

Walking from the dark hallway into the bright kitchen made her flinch just a little, and before she knew it, Deon was jumping up from his chair to kiss her forehead and wrap his arms around her.

"Are you okay, baby?" he asked.

She smiled up at him and nodded.

Naomi was immediately on alert by Deon's question and looked at Stella in alarm. "Did something happen?"

Everyone in the kitchen stopped to look at Stella and Deon. Jake was leaning back against the kitchen counter wearing his usual jeans and a t-shirt. He'd grown a beard since joining the Fines Creek community. Stella had always known Jake was meant to be in the mountains. Naomi was still in her scrubs from a day at work as a hygienist. They may live off the grid, but most people in Fines Creek had the healthiest teeth of any outsider community. Next to Naomi was Ocean, in old but decent and clean clothes. Was it really a year and a half ago that she found Ocean, almost dead, in a gas station? It seemed like both yesterday and much too long ago. Ocean was sitting quietly as always, with her hands folded and on the table. Sitting at the table was a woman who Stella had never seen before. She had sharp features and her hair was pulled into a tight ponytail.

"Chris, the wheat farmer . . . his wife died on my table today of a heart attack," Stella said, unsure of sharing such information in a stranger's presence.

"Oh, I'm so sorry," Naomi replied, frowning. If they'd been alone, Stella knew Naomi would have offered a hug, but with Deon's arms already around her, just knowing that her friend was there was enough.

Jake looked up at the ceiling and blinked a few times. The biggest fear of any outsider was not having the health services that the live-work communities had. They feared not making it to the doctor on time because all the hospitals were closed or that the only doctor available didn't have the skill set required, such as fertility treatments and transplants.

Stella directed her attention to the woman sitting at the table with Naomi. "Hi, I don't think we've met. I'm Stella." She offered her hand.

The woman stood and shook her hand. "No, ma'am, we haven't. I'm Amy. I've worked with Jake before, ma'am."

Military through and through. "So, is something going on?"

"Yes, ma'am, have you heard of the cleansing initiative?"

"Yes, we did hear about that."

"Well, it's fully launched, ma'am. Now, they're coming for all outsiders."

"You mean, for us? For everyone? Whether or not we're hostile?"

"Yes, ma'am, that's what I'm saying."

Stella shook her head. "And how is it that you know we're here?"

Jake stepped forward. "She's, uh, been in touch with me."

"You told her we were here?" Stella asked. It wasn't meant as an accusation but more of a curiosity. It'd never occurred to her before that their location should be secret or that they should have been taking precautions to hide.

"Ma'am, the drones have been reporting back the locations of all outsider communities. We currently know of over two hundred. Fines Creek has developed into one of the larger communities." Amy looked flushed, as though it was embarrassing that she'd been in touch with Jake. Stella noticed that Naomi looked away from Amy as she blushed to save her the dignity.

"She's been providing information from the inside for us. She's how we knew about the cleansing," Jake offered.

"Thank you for that information. But why are you helping us?" Stella asked.

"I've got a brother that's an outsider. In fact, he's my next stop, and I want to make it there tonight, so I've got to get going. It was nice to meet you, ma'am." Amy stood and stuck her hand out to shake Stella's. Stella took it and smiled at Amy, thanking her one more time. Amy then shook Deon's hand, and she blushed as she reached to Naomi to shake her hand. She and Jake shared a quick shake before she exited the kitchen, Jake and Deon following her.

Stella raised her eyebrows toward Naomi, who laughed. Stella sat down and Naomi reached for the whiskey and poured Stella a shot. Naomi and Stella both preferred wine, but truth be told, the men were better at making whiskey than wine. From the front of the house, they heard the men say goodbye to Amy and the door shut. Only a few seconds later, Deon's voice boomed down the hall, "She's got a little crush on you, Jake!"

The women laughed, knowing Jake wouldn't appreciate the observation. Stella could imagine he'd blush just as much as Amy did a moment ago. Both women purposefully hid their laughter when the men walked back into the kitchen, but when Naomi made eye contact with Jake, the jig was up, and she burst out laughing again.

"So, do I need to be worried about your little informant?" Naomi teased, cutting her eyes up toward him as though she was flirting.

"You know she's not my type." Jake blushed just as Stella thought he would.

Deon laughed and dug his knuckles into Jake's arm. "Just giving you a hard time, man."

Jake nodded his head in appreciation. "Seriously, though, she didn't know when they're launching or where they're starting, but given that we have one of the largest outsider communities, I'd guess we're top of the list, so we need to be ready."

"I'm going to be honest; I think we need help," Deon said.

"Who are you thinking?" Jake asked.

"Some good friends. Some exceptionally good friends. But it won't be easy to get them here."

Jake looked sideways at Deon. "Are you meaning . . ."

"Yup, that's who I mean," Deon replied.

"And we need to convince Fines Creek to prepare for war," Jake stated, looking at Stella.

"You leave that to me. I'll call a town hall and let them know what needs to be done," Stella replied.

"Stella, I don't doubt you. Never have and never will. But it won't be easy to get a community of farmers to become soldiers," Naomi said.

"It's a good thing we've got so many ex-military here to help," Ocean said.

Stella pointed a finger toward Ocean. "And that's exactly what's going to give us an advantage. We have something to defend, something to fight for. They couldn't take it away when their businesses packed up and left town, and they can't take it away now. It's not their right to take away what is ours. They will not strip us of citizen scores and then blame us for it." Stella was standing by the time she finished.

"And that, baby, is why everyone will listen to you," Deon said as he wrapped her up again in his arms.

FRIDAY | JUNE 9, 2073

MILES

A change was coming, and the dupes were buzzing about it even though the rumors hadn't been confirmed. They knew their assignment in New York was coming to an end soon. And though some would remain to protect the bridges from outsiders crossing and attacking New York, it wasn't nearly as much of an effort to protect New York as, say, Sacramento. Most of them would be reassigned off the grid, taking out the number one threat of civilians: the outsiders.

They had a lot more freedom than they'd had in training. Now, they could go and visit friends, play cards, or even fuck. But those weren't the type of things that was on Miles' mind. He had a war to fight, and not on the side of the United States. His only choice was to escape, start his own army, and recruit the very people his own kind had been brainwashed to kill.

Soon, the new assignments would be given, and he realized this was their chance to get out without raising too much suspicion. That meant talking to Leticia as soon as possible, and what better time did he have than now? Losing

HABITUAL HUMANITY

sleep was an easy choice, but he'd have to be quiet so as not to wake anyone or gain the attention of their superiors.

He got out of his bunk, which thankfully he shared with Zac, his brother, who wouldn't give a shit, and quietly exited their room. Miles wound his way through a series of halls of tiny apartments meant for one but which had two soldiers assigned to each. He exited the building and went down the street, past several buildings with the same setup, and into the military living quarters that were closest to the city and, therefore, had the best view.

The elevators were purposefully turned off in all buildings, forcing them to exercise even when they simply needed to go get something to eat. He had to hand it to the military, as all the dupes were covered in muscle. He hadn't seen a single original, as they'd come to think of people that weren't dupes, even come close to the fitness of a dupe—unless he counted those so-called muscle builders, but that just seemed like a ridiculous thing to do to oneself. He took the stairs to the twentieth floor and turned down the corridor to Leticia's tiny apartment, giving her door a soft knock.

Leticia's roommate opened the door, hair in a bun on top of her head with loose strands sticking out in every direction and eyes half-closed.

"Sorry if I woke you—" Miles started, but she cut him off.

"Yeah, ya did. It's midnight, what the fuck do you want?"

"Leticia," Miles said simply.

The woman turned from the door and retreated to her bed. The apartments were so tiny, the bed was only about twenty feet away. On the top bunk was Leticia, who sat up and squinted as she eyed the door.

"Hey," Leticia said in a gruff voice, and then she noisily cleared her throat. Without another word, she descended the short ladder and joined him in the hall, still in her military assigned pajamas of light gray pants and shirt.

"Is there anywhere we can go to talk?" Miles asked.

"The break area." She guided him through the building until they came to a room with a few plastic chairs around tables and an empty counter along the longest wall. Other than the two of them, no one was there. She sat down at a table that was farthest from the door and overlooking Water Street.

"I'm sure you've heard the rumor we're about to be reassigned," Miles started.

"Yup," Leticia nodded. She rubbed her eyes and leaned back in her chair.

"It's time we make our own assignments. We're going back to Miller Base, and I need for you to be sure that it happens."

Her eyes shot open. "Our training base? The one they closed down?"

"You got it."

"No problem with getting *us* rerouted to Miller Base, but if we and all of our recruits are reassigned there, it's going to raise some red flags." She raised her eyebrows.

"Send some soldiers to temporary locations before informing them to head to Miller Base."

"Got it, brother. But how are we going to get more recruits? Miller Base isn't exactly going to be crawling with potential candidates. We don't have enough people; it's not time."

Miles looked Leticia in the eye and leaned forward. "It *is* time. We've recruited enough for a good start, and they're going to start reassigning most of us. If we don't use this opportunity to our advantage, then the only choice left for us will be to go AWOL—and that'll gain too much attention. *Now* is the time." He held his position, looking her in the eye, but his expression was soft and understanding. "Let's get our brothers and sisters safely there, then we'll figure out the numbers."

"Yes, sir."

Miles got up to leave, but then stopped short and turned back toward her. "I need Andrei to do something, too. You

HABITUAL HUMANITY

see him, right? He's in your unit?"

"Yup, I'll see him tomorrow. What do we need to do?"

"Have Andrei start sending supplies to Miller Base. I don't want you constantly in the system, so you two should share the work. That way if one of you gets caught, they won't know the extent of it."

"You want us to move people *and* guns, and somehow keep it under the radar?"

"I want you to move people, guns, Jeeps, and food, plus any other supplies we'll need. But the military will also be moving supplies for all the changes in assignments, and with all the moving parts, we have a better chance of doing it undetected."

Leticia smiled and nodded. "Yes, sir. We'll get it done."

FRIDAY | JUNE 9, 2073

AUGUST PAXTON

August woke to the sound of his satellite phone ringing. He and Darius had already had their usual early call, and Darius rarely called him twice in the same morning. August sat up immediately, frantically reaching between his mattresses, thinking he wouldn't get it in time. As soon as his hand touched it, he yanked it out and tapped the screen.

"Hello again!"

The sound of a long breath came over the line, and then Darius said, "You need to get out of Laurel."

"What do you mean?"

"The cleansing is going full scale. They're going after all outsiders." The sound of his breath quickened; he must have been walking while talking. Darius never used the secret phone anywhere but in his bedroom. A feeling of dread filled August, like blood was rushing out of his head. The sadness in Darius' voice was deep and hollow in a way he'd never heard it before. "How do you know this?"

"I—" Darius paused and swallowed. "I've never told you this, but I'm a part of the team that creates the clones. And now they're launching the cleansing initiative full scale to exterminate outsiders."

"You what?" August almost yelled the words. He stood up out of bed and began to pace the room.

Darius was silent for a minute. August could picture him closing his eyes, not wanting to reiterate what he'd just admitted. "I made them, August. I'm one of the scientists in charge of the clone army creation, and you need to get out. They'll be ruthless. Don't worry about anyone else, just you."

"What are you saying? What does an endocrinologist have to do with building some super army of clones?" August rubbed his forehead as he tried to wrap his brain around the news.

The door to his room opened and Audrey, with seemingly permanent black circles under her eyes after her ordeal in Sacramento, poked her head in. "Is everything okay?"

August waved a dismissive hand toward her.

"I work with a geneticist, a pediatrician, two engineers, and their teams to make dupes. Specifically, I modify their hormones for aggressiveness as well as other characteristics."

August stood still, breathing hard. He was holding back, but he wasn't sure what it was he holding back. Yelling? Crying? Audrey fully entered his room, and he could feel her eyes on him. He shook his head to indicate that he wasn't going to want to talk anytime soon.

On the phone, Darius continued, "I wasn't allowed to tell you. But then, after the news became public, the secret had gone on for too long, and I was afraid you'd hate me for it. I didn't have the heart to tell you the truth."

August glanced sideways at Audrey and tilted his head vigorously several times toward the door before turning away from her. "Let me get this straight. Your real job is to modify humans to become Blakes and Luckys?" August needed to hear it bluntly, because there was no way that the man he loved would do such an unforgivable thing. Both had a hard time recovering from the murders they witnessed in the Wastebasket, and both still had nightmares. There was no way his boyfriend was part of the team responsible for creating that horror again.

When Darius didn't respond, it was more than enough. "What the fuck?" August yelled into the phone. He'd never spoken to Darius like that before, and he immediately hated himself. His hands were shaking, and he had to ball his free hand into a fist to get it to stop. Then he realized that Audrey was still standing in his doorway, her eyes wide and full of fear. August slumped his shoulders in guilt, heartbreak, and agitation. He waved his hand at her trying to say, *This isn't your argument, leave.* But she was as stubborn as she'd been growing up, and she shook her head in response.

Darius' voice finally came over the phone again. "I'm telling you now because you need to know they're coming for you, all of you. You need to get out."

August resumed pacing the length of his room. "I hear what you're saying, but I'm still confused—you'd rather create serial killers than to be with me?"

There was nothing but silence on the other end of the phone.

"Thanks for the heads up." August hung up without waiting for a response.

MONDAY | JUNE 12, 2073

MILES

On the edge of New York City, in a building that had been intended for for international conferences, the dupes gathered in a large room that, in a previous life, had been adorned with large screens, multi-colored lights, and massive speakers. For the dupes, there were only two simple screens, one for the crowd in the front half of the room and the other for the back half. Two small speakers were placed on the stage, one on each side of a plain wooden podium, while the dupes sat and waited for the meeting to begin. The room no longer contained the curtains that had previously hidden the back portion of the room where, supposedly, magic happened. The bare bones of the equipment from another life of parties and large meetings were left in the dark, like the bones of a corpse.

Miles sat with Zac, Leticia, Asim, and Andrei in the middle of the giant echoing room as one of their superiors, whom none of them recognized, repeated the word "test." Each time, his voice sent a crackling through the tiny and insufficient speakers. Other superiors twisted random knobs but shrugged their shoulders when the crackling persisted.

HABITUAL HUMANITY

Miles sat forward, took a deep breath, and then twisted in his seat just enough to look around them. Some friends nodded acknowledgments, and Miles nodded in return.

Miles felt the knot in his stomach tighten. If they'd planned their escape well, they'd be on their way back to Tennessee in a few days without any superior wiser as to what was going on. If not, their new assignments to a closed-down base would be announced in front of the thousands present, and there was no doubt that the punishment would be execution. His strategy would either give his siblings freedom or cost them their lives.

Did Mother realize this would be the level of his burden? Did she realize the cost? Was this plan implanted into him like the plans into the other dupes? A little tweak of DNA and he was never able to make his own choice?

"Find a seat. We'll begin soon," the testing superior announced. The last few dupes flowed into the room and sat down.

Miles put his head in his hands. His heart slammed against his ribcage with each beat, but he still had to behave like a dupe, so he sat back in his chair as though he was just another soldier excited to learn of his next assignment.

"Good morning, everyone," said a different and yet again unfamiliar superior. In a flat tone, she continued, "According to our data, we've eradicated ninety-eight percent of the outsiders from New York City. With New York City secured, proving we can provide a safe live-work community for citizens, we can move onto the bigger threat." The superior shuffled some papers, looking off to the side of the stage as though she was looking for someone.

After a few minutes, another superior walked onto the stage, took the podium, and began to speak. "As you know, the outsiders have been a major concern for the United States. Their numbers grow almost daily, and now they're using new tactics to try to bring harm to the citizens and government of the United States. There has been a hack on the citizen data, which is going to have a substantial impact

HABITUAL HUMANITY

on our system of credit. It is your job to ensure this doesn't happen again. Please watch the screens for your names to find out where your assignment is and where to report tomorrow."

The two screens lit up and showed in plain text, "Montana, Buses 1 - 10." The next few screens displayed a list of names that did not include Miles or his siblings. As the soldiers listed left the room, everyone waited. Then another assignment appeared, this time reading, "Sacramento, Buses 11-25." Again, several screens showed a list of names, and again, there was a mass exit of dupes. Miles and his siblings were not on this list either. It took hours to get through all the assignments, but at the end, Miles was not listed on any of the assignments, nor were any of his brothers or sisters. They stood with the last group, a few of them looking around as if to see if anyone noticed their names hadn't been on the list at all. They walked out together with the dupes on the last given assignment, and as they did, Miles released a deep breath.

"I didn't think it would work," Asim said, running a hand through his hair.

"You doubted me?" Leticia replied, raising an eyebrow.

"I don't doubt you, sis, but that was a tough one."

"Agreed. Thank you, Leticia," Miles said with a small smile and a nod toward Leticia. Outside the massive room, in an equally massive hallway, many of the dupes gathered and chatted about their assignments, which provided a perfect cover for his crew to do the same.

"Now what do we do?" Zac asked Miles.

"That's for me to answer," Letica said. "Tomorrow, you—" she pointed at Miles, Asim, and Andrei "—go to Oklahoma's buses, but *be late*. There will be one broken-down bus, and that will be ours."

"You are a genius, assuming the bus isn't actually broken down." Asim winked at Leticia.

She smirked and replied, "I'll leave you in suspense."

"What about our other brothers and sisters?" Andrei

asked.

"Mattie, Khloe, Ramone, and Tala are recruiting in their own bases," Miles replied. "They, and those they've recruited, are being routed through various cities and will eventually meet us there. It will take time, but that way we're harder to trace." Miles turned his attention to Andrei and asked, "How are the supplies coming?"

"Slow. I can't add new vendors without attracting attention, so the only way to stay under the radar is with small shipments, and not too many at once. Weapons and a two-photon laser will be the hardest supplies to get a hold of, but I'm working on it."

"Thank you, both," Miles said as he nodded toward Leticia and Andrei. "Zac and Leticia are staying behind to be our informants and keep inside the system." Miles looked directly at both of them and added, "Be careful, and don't take chances. Everyone else get packed. Meet tomorrow with the Oklahoma crew."

The group dispersed, hugging or slapping the backs of Zac and Leticia before heading toward their apartments. Miles and Zac walked together to their shared apartment.

"Dude, you alright?" Zac asked.

"Yeah, I'm good."

"Liar. You're going to miss me a shit ton!"

Miles stopped suddenly and stared at Zac. Would this be the last time he saw his brother?

"We've been dealt a shitty hand, brother, but at least we have each other." Zac flashed a cheesy grin, wrapped his arm around Miles' back, and they headed back to their building for what would be the last night they were American soldiers.

THURSDAY | JUNE 15, 2073

GENERAL MAXWELL

The maps displayed within a control room of the Pentagon turned red in multiple locations across the United States. Each red dot had a number above it ranging from one to ten thousand, and more red dots with numbers kept appearing by the minute.

The room was a semicircle of desks all facing toward the wall of maps. There was a collective cheer from those within the room, excited that the drone test to identify outsider locations and inform the military units with up-to-date information seemed successful.

A short, round man yelled to the group over the cheering, "Check with the battalions! Can they see what we see?"

The room fell silent as everyone returned to their computers to check with their assigned military units.

"Confirmed, sir. They can see what we can see," a young intern confirmed.

The rest of the room resumed cheering while the round man frowned.

"What's the matter, Mr. Sanders? Success isn't good

HABITUAL HUMANITY

enough for you?" General Maxwell asked with a big grin across his face. "I put a difficult task on your team, to execute custom drones, develop programs, and obtain a lot of equipment for this war. I know it was difficult, but it's the first like it in history. And nothing meant for history is ever easy. You and I," General Maxwell said, then turning toward the room and raising his voice, "and your fantastic team have changed the way wars are won!"

Everyone in the room applauded, but not Mr. Sanders. "I'm ecstatic, sir," Mr. Sanders replied, monotone, without a hint of joy on his face.

General Maxwell turned and walked out of the room in a few long strides. He reached into his pocket, pulling out his cell phone, and dialed a phone number only a handful of those in the world had access to.

"Yes, General?" President Wood said when she answered.

"The drones are up and working. The deployed units also have a visual of the data. We are ready to deploy on your command," General Maxwell said as he looked out of the windows of the Pentagon that overlooked the cantilevered benches built in honor of the attack on September 11 so long ago. The structures emitted a yellow light like marigolds and were especially beautiful in the setting sun.

"Thank you, General. Operation Great Eye is a go. Be here within the hour for a press conference."

"Yes, ma'am," the general responded. Holding the phone away from his face, he watched the screen turn dark before pivoting on his heel and returning to his team.

It was the beginning of the end. He'd be a part of the operation that would bring the United States together again, and what better accomplishment could he have been a part of? It hadn't been easy to live in the United States during a time when so much had been lost, and it'd been difficult to keep the citizens safe, but it would be worth it to see it all merge once again.

Back inside the war room, he raised his voice to ensure

all within could hear him. "It was your job to find all the outsider locations, and you did that. And you did an excellent job. Now it's the military's job to turn those numbers into zeros. Operation Great Eye is a go!" Then he leaned over into Mr. Sanders' ear and whispered, "If anything goes wrong, I'll have your ass."

"I know, sir," Mr. Sanders responded, shrinking like a turtle inside of his light-blue collared shirt. Mr. Sanders turned his attention to the room. "Pass the controls to the operators! Be available if they need anything. And I do mean *anything*."

Heads immediately turned down and fingers started tapping. The battalions across the United States were gearing up and readying to head into the outside. War was now, and it felt good to General Maxwell to watch the solution in action.

He left the room once again, leaving Mr. Sanders in charge, and rushed down a few corridors and up a flight of stairs before emerging onto the roof of the Pentagon where a helicopter was waiting for him. The ride would only take a few minutes, but there were no minutes to spare. As soon as it landed on the White House lawn, he was escorted to the White House Rose Garden where soldiers stepped aside to allow him to pass without question. President Danica Wood, surrounded by her immediate staff, smiled when he entered the lawn. A crowd of reporters immediately began reporting her reaction into their cameras as the general took his place by her side.

None of the news stations had been informed of what the press conference would be for. There was a constant buzz of speculation from the reporters who were digging for anything, good information or outright blatant lie, that would help them have a leg up on the news. News consumption was born and dead within minutes, and if a station wasn't the first to report it, their stock would plummet in one day. You were either first, or nothing. So, when the press secretary walked onto the stage, a dead silence fell upon the reporters.

"The President will speak in five minutes."

The cameramen rushed to double-check their settings, and news reporters took positions and straightened their jackets. In exactly four minutes and fifty-five seconds, the press secretary took the stage once again.

"Ladies and gentlemen, the President."

President Wood stepped onto the stage with her short gray hair and expression that always looked particularly stern. Before she spoke into the microphone, she flashed a thin smile that didn't reach her eyes. The plan to eradicate the United States of all the outsiders had been difficult to design, and she'd gotten very little sleep over the past month. She took a moment to look each reporter in the eye to let them know that this was going to be the story of the year.

"For the past few decades, history has been made for us. The economy crashed, jobs were lost, even food has been scarce in our great country. Solutions take time, and we've taken that time. We've worked hard to eradicate ourselves of these problems by developing live-work communities as well as the Utopias to keep our citizens safe and healthy. And last year, you re-elected me because you believed in my ability to bring America together again. And today, I'm proud to share with you, the American people, that we're launching the final step that will bring America back to her full glory."

President Wood paused and glanced around the room before continuing. "Right now, over 250,000 troops within the United States are deploying. No, we're not attacking China, or Germany, or Russia. We're marching on the number one enemy of U.S. citizens: the outsiders."

She paused again, allowing her words to sink in. She waited until the frantic scribbling slowed to a stall.

"Today is a day that will go down in history. This is the day we stop being reactive and we start being proactive. Today we stop the defense and we begin our offense. We stop responding to the conversation and start initiating the conversation. Today, we are the peacemakers.

"Martial law has been in effect in America for almost a full decade. For part of that time, there's been no respite for those that chose not to be a part of the solution. Without everyone, we've not been able to work together to rebuild. We've not worked together to ask, 'What could we be? What about our children's future?' The only legacy we can leave behind is what we did as a nation to make tomorrow better and brighter. Without their help, we've built the best future we could. We've worked hard for our economy. We've labored to rebuild our military. And now, we're stronger."

President Wood smiled, and this time it reached her eyes. "And today, we launch that military on them. We will reinforce martial law to its fullest. The curfew, outside of the live-work communities, will be eight p.m. Anyone caught outside past eight p.m. will be shot on sight. Please do not make a fatal mistake of assuming the soldiers will not shoot—I assure you they will. If an outsider wants to reinstate their citizenship, then all the individual needs to do is pay their back taxes." President Wood once again paused, nodding her head as if to agree with herself.

"Thank you for your time today and thank you to all Americans who have never turned their backs on the American dream, on what we are and will be. We'll once again be the most advanced country in this world. We will be the ideal of all other countries and the precipice that they will strive to be. This is the presidency that will unite America again!"

President Wood turned and with a perfectly straight back walked off the stage, into the White House, and into the Oval Office with General Maxwell on her heels. As they entered the Oval Office, they shut the door behind them.

President Wood, once she was behind her thick ornate wood desk, turned toward General Maxwell and said, "Thank you, General, you've done a good job."

"Thank you, Madame President, that means a lot to me."

"Any word on Admiral Herbert?" She sat in her large leather chair.

HABITUAL HUMANITY

"No, ma'am, I dare say at this point I'm afraid we may not find him," General Maxwell replied. Out of all he could do successfully for his country, this was one thing he hadn't been able to accomplish. It was as though Admiral Herbert had just vanished. Sometimes General Maxwell was convinced they had it all wrong, that Admiral Herbert wasn't AWOL but simply missing. No one could disappear, vanish, and leave no trace behind. But then that left the mystery of his son, Captain Herbert. Could both of them just vanish? It seemed just as unlikely that two of the most formidable men ever to be known in the military would both be murdered and buried without a trace of foul play. Both scenarios were unlikely, and that irked him. It made him look like he didn't have a clue what he was doing. But, he had to remind himself, it also meant that no one else could do any better. He had his best people on the job.

"How is it that an admiral and a captain can just go missing?" President Wood raised her hands in the air as though she was wafting away smoke.

General Maxwell took a quick breath at her comment. There was something about this woman that made him want to impress her. "I'm going to find that out, ma'am. And Operation Great Eye is perfect timing, just the thing we need to help root them out."

"I hope so, general. You're dismissed."

General Maxwell pivoted and exited the room. The President was a small woman, only five foot four, but she was the only one that could make him feel like he was only two feet tall.

SATURDAY | JUNE 17, 2073

AUGUST PAXTON

August got up and walked into the kitchen, his large feet unintentionally pounding on the hardwood floors. He was no longer the lanky teenager that had worked on the Minko, he was a broad-shouldered man with a full beard. His sister, Audrey, who looked a lot like him but with longer hair and the pointier jawline of their mother, sat at the kitchen table.

"Can you check the news?" August asked.

"Looking for news on the cleansing again?"

"Yup. In fact, look for news on New York."

"New York? I don't mean to be cold, but why are you worried about that? It's not a good thing, but there's nothing we can do."

August scratched his head, trying to determine how much to tell her. "It's beyond New York now."

"Can you please tell me who was on the phone?" Audrey asked. She'd been trying to get information out of August since she listened in on his phone call. August avoided the topic at any cost, but since he wasn't talking to Darius and couldn't ask for more information, he'd asked her to look for

HABITUAL HUMANITY

news, and now she was cornering him. August still didn't want to share the information that Darius had given him. First, he didn't want Audrey to worry, but second, it hurt too damn bad.

"Can you just look? No questions, alright?" August pleaded. It was his only chance to get around her stubborn side.

She typed away at the laptop. August couldn't stand not doing anything, so he stepped away and retrieved coffee beans from a cabinet. As he plugged in the grinder, a use of electricity that Audrey insisted was wasteful, he contemplated how much longer they'd have coffee. Their supplier and partner in trade had gone silent over the past few months, and an oncoming war would make all trade difficult if not impossible. The high pitch of the tiny engine crunching the coffee beans filled the room, so he didn't realize Audrey had stopped typing. He poured the grinds into the coffee maker and filled it with water, hitting the brew button. Spinning around, he saw that Audrey's face had gone blank.

"Audrey, what is it?" August asked. He stepped forward and put his hands on her shoulders. "Show me," he said in a soft tone.

Audrey moved the laptop so that the screen faced August.

On the screen, President Wood stood in front of a group of reporters. " This is the presidency that will unite America again!"

"In the article, it says the troops were being deployed as she made the announcement and that we can just pay our back taxes and get our citizenships back," Audrey said. "Do you think she's telling the truth, that if we just pay taxes it'll all be alright? Like when our parents were young?"

"I've seen these guys in action, and they don't give a shit about anyone. Even if you're holding a baby, don't think they won't shoot." August's face was bright red, remembering the events that he witnessed in the Wastebasket. There was no way he was trusting those soldiers with his community.

"How long before they get here?" Audrey asked.

"I don't know. How can we know?"

A humming distracted them from the conversation, and they both rushed to the window to see. Seeing nothing, they rushed out of their front door and onto the front porch just in time to see a giant drone speeding past their farm and on down toward the Miller's.

"So that's how they're doing it," August said.

"What?" Audrey asked with a wide-eyed, panicked expression that almost seemed permanent in her eyes.

"The drones will collect data on how many people are here. That's how the soldiers will know where to go. They'll probably attack the biggest populations first."

"So, we have no chance?" Audrey said, swallowing.

"Never say that." August turned and ran toward the computer. He brought up the chat system they'd created for their community and sent a message to every household that it was time to either pick up their arms or hide in their shelters. After sending the message, he secured two pistols on his waist and slid the strap of his rifle over his torso.

"Come on, you're going into the shelter," August said as he grabbed her arm and headed out the door.

"No!" Audrey yanked her arm from his grip. "There's no way I'm not fighting."

"I need to keep you safe," August urged.

"I watched my apartment building go up in flames. I couldn't help our parents at all. I couldn't do anything!" Tears streaked her face again. "You can't just lock me up! I have to be a part of this!" Audrey stalked off to her room and came back with an assault rifle.

August was shocked to see his peaceful, animal-loving, vegetarian sister holding a weapon. "Do you know how to use that? Or, tell me this, is the safety on?"

Audrey adjusted the gun to hold it in both of her hands, making August duck to stay out of its aim.

"This is against my better judgment," August said as

reached over to touch the tiny lever that prevented the trigger from being pulled. "That's the safety."

Audrey's eyebrows furled and her tears stopped. "If you need to see me cold and hard to believe I can fight, here you go. But just because a few tears come down doesn't mean I'm not strong."

August laughed. "Oh, I know you're strong, I just don't know if I trust you with *that*. I'll teach you how to use a pistol later." He turned toward the front door, pushing it partially open, but then he turned back and added, "Love you, sis."

"Love you, too. Now, let's kick some ass."

SATURDAY | JUNE 17, 2073

AUGUST PAXTON

August and Audrey drove to what was called Central Point, which used to be a Super Center before the businesses closed shop and left town. There were multiple families already there. The normally quiet town was full of the sounds of engines as more families drove in. They reserved using gas for emergency meetings, so the noise was loud compared to the quiet that usually filled the town. Close to a hundred families had answered August's call to meet at the gathering point. It was early morning, and messages sometimes took time to reach everyone, so August could depend on many more joining the fight.

August jumped up on the back of his old baby-blue Chevy truck and listened for the sound of more engines and horses approaching. Hearing mostly silence, he took it as a sign to get started.

"The President has announced a cleansing of outsiders. They're imposing a curfew on us and sending the army!"

Murmuring broke out among the group, and Josh Miller spoke up above the rest. "If we work with them, then maybe things will get better."

"This isn't an army of soldiers, it's an army of dupes. And they're not coming for peace. That's not what they're trained to do." August swallowed, trying to keep the emotions of his post-traumatic stress at bay as well as his fight with Darius.

"But what if working with them would bring jobs and food?" Josh jumped up on his own truck, creating a loud thud. "Sure, we'd have to figure out the taxes, and sure, we'd have to be home by what, seven or eight p.m.? It's not like we're going to the movies or to the high school football game. We need the government to give us back a thriving economy. This is our chance to give our children the type of life that, right now, is nothing more than a story of the past."

"That's not what they're bringing. This is an army developed for brute force, modified to take and execute orders at any cost. An army trained to kill a child as fast as they'd kill a full-grown man. They won't care about your children. They won't care about your land. They know we no longer have American money. That's why it's the option. It looks like they're being empathic when they know it's not possible," August yelled out.

Before August could finish, Josh spoke again. "Maybe we can start a trade, just like we've done here! That's how we earn the money for the taxes!" Josh spat as he spoke.

"You need to hide your children and pick up your guns," August demanded in a low but powerful tone, staring Josh in the eye.

"Those who want peace, stand up!" Josh yelled out, raising his fist. A few people raised their fists in response.

August didn't like how this was turning out, and he was sure they were going to die. "They're not coming because they respect you. They're coming to kill you. You need to hide your children and prepare to fight for what is yours!"

Half of the families hooped and hollered in response. The loud sound of a collective group felt good, infectious to August. But that meant half of the families were staying quiet, either not sure or hoping the way to freedom didn't include violence. And half wasn't near enough to win a battle like the one coming their way.

Marshall Bird, who August had had several classes with in high school, spoke up. "What if they kill our families because we don't comply?"

"What if you comply and never have a chance to see your family again?" August asked.

"How do we know that what you're saying is true?" Marshall asked.

"I saw these men when I served. They were the reason I left, why I went AWOL. I joined the military for a chance at freedom, for a chance at wealth and health insurance. Instead, I saw them kill people for *target practice*." August closed his eyes at the memory and had to wait before speaking again. "We can't trust them. This is a war on us because they—" August pointed his finger towards the east "—abandoned us when times got hard. They left us to our own devices. And we made it! We made this work! We took care of our kids. Okay, so we don't have football games, but don't the kids get together and play football in your fields, Jerry?"

"Yup, sure do," Jerry responded.

"And who's winning?"

"The white shirts," Jerry responded with a smile.

"The white shirts are winning. And how many times have the little children gathered at your house to watch those old cartoon movies on that sheet hanging in your yard, Hanna?"

"I've lost count," Hanna responded with a chuckle.

"And now they want to take even that away from us. And what threat do we pose? What has the town of Laurel done to deserve a unit marching on it? *Nothing*."

A murmuring erupted across the crowd.

"Stand with me and fight. Fight for our right to freedom. Fight for our football games and movies. Fight for your children. Fight for the right to live!"

The crowd exploded in a loud cheer.

SATURDAY | JUNE 17, 2073

STELLA HOPKINS

The town hall meeting couldn't be put off. Stella always felt stronger with Deon by her side, but the community of Fines Creek needed to come together, and the greater good of the whole outweighed her personal wishes.

Opening one of the solid oak doors of the old church, now used as a town hall, it struck her as odd that she seemed to be highly regarded by the community. Even some that had originally shunned her and had made it clear she wasn't welcome, frequently sought her advice. And now that the rumor had spread like wildfire that a war was coming, emotions were high and people were looking to her for guidance. If she didn't pull people together now, Fines Creek could fall apart.

She stood in the middle of the oval room they used for meetings. The actual town hall building wasn't that large, and it hadn't drawn that big of a crowd when Fines Creek was still a part of the American economy. As soon as the livelihood was taken away, those that had never been involved in politics became extremely involved. It was a shame that it was too late to save the town. Nonetheless, they needed a bigger spot to start gathering, and the church finally got the attendance it'd always pined for, only for the wrong reasons.

She stepped onto the blue-carpeted platform that Stella had learned was almost as old as the town itself. It looked how she felt, worn and old, but hopefully she smelled better than the dank musk it gave off. It would be nice if they could have a better gathering place, just as it would to have a house that represented her style, but such things had become trivial. The ceiling and walls were intact, and they could heat and cool the place enough to make the meeting bearable. She closed her eyes and recited her prepared speech in her mind. This wasn't going to be easy.

The first of the families entered the old church, and Stella approached them with a smile and a hello. Their frowns and slumped shoulders made it clear the worry they brought was impenetrable. Her arms ached to take it away. She wanted to say she had an answer, but the truth was, there was never a right answer in times such as these. She knew this now. The young, confident version of herself that would have thought she'd had the answers was gone, and in her place was a woman with experience, disappointment, and too much knowledge to play that card now.

More people entered, and she greeted them as well, but not a single person had the usual friendly demeanor. No one smiled or discussed crops, trade expansion, or families. Dread filled Stella that this town meeting would take an awful turn, that this day, in only a few minutes, would change Fines Creek forever.

Nothing ever stayed the same. Life wasn't at all what she'd wanted or envisioned, not even close. But worse than losing her own dreams was losing the ones she'd held on to for Jevan. Today was no different than all the other hits she'd taken, and the only element within her control was to keep her family together, keep moving forward, and keep making the best of it.

HABITUAL HUMANITY

She straightened her back. No matter what everyone chose, it would be their choice. And that's what was important, that everyone had their right to choose. She'd have to add the hope, so she smiled.

Just then, Ocean entered the room. Stella released a breath she hadn't realized she was holding. Ocean was a beam of light, and Stella couldn't believe that she'd come across the girl on that fateful day. Stella had wanted more children, and Ocean, even though she was pretty much grown, had filled her heart in a way she'd never known could happen.

Stella opened her arms and wrapped them around Ocean, who returned the embrace.

"Will you join me on the platform?" Stella asked. It was unfair to ask the girl to be her strength, and she regretted it immediately.

"I don't think I could get up there." Ocean shook her head.

"You can sit in the front row then, if you like."

Ocean nodded. She was such a bright girl, and Stella had enjoyed taking her under her wing. She was also very shy and never wanted to be the center of attention. Not that Stella viewed that as bad—certainly not everyone had to be gregarious—but she worried it would hold Ocean back.

"Everyone looks so sad," Ocean observed.

"They have reason to be sad."

"No matter where anyone goes, there's something bad happening. It's hard to understand why we can't just all live in peace."

"Agreed. We must not let it stop us from working toward peace."

Ocean nodded and gave Stella a quick smile before moving toward the front pew to sit.

The church had almost filled during their conversation, and Stella smiled at all the beautiful families that sat beside their neighbors. Fines Creek wasn't perfect, but there was a community here that loved their children and their neighbors. What more could she or anyone strive for?

She walked up to the platform and stood in the middle.

"Thank you for coming," she said, projecting her voice as far as she could. The room quieted quickly as everyone looked up at her. A sea of pensive expressions looking for answers looked up at her. "Outsiders have destroyed the barrier in Sacramento, and there have been attacks on other live-work communities. The citizens are scared that outsiders are banding together in coordinated attacks. We've received information that the army is indeed marching upon outsiders, and whether or not we're a part of the outside planned initiative, war *is* upon us."

She waited only a moment to let the community digest what she just shared, and then quickly started speaking again, afraid that panic would control the meeting rather than her if she didn't stand tall.

"Now, we have a choice. We must choose if we're going to stay and fight, or leave. We must choose what is best for our families."

One of the men stood and called out, "I don't think there is a choice. We must fight!"

"Yes, there is a choice; I want my children to be safe!" a woman responded.

Stella valued making her own choices above anything, and therefore never wanted to make a decision on behalf of the community. But as more people joined in the argument, she realized that giving a choice in such a large public platform wasn't a good idea.

"Now!" she called out, raising her voice even higher and feeling it threatening to crack. "We have people who can train us to fight. We have the capability to fight back. We will have a better chance of protecting our community if we choose to work together!" It was too late to inspire them all after telling them they had a choice to run, but it was better than never having said it at all.

"But we're one community, and it's an entire army!" called out one of the men. "*Maybe* we can win the first attack, but that doesn't mean we'll survive a second or third. They won't stop until they wipe us out!"

Stella began to speak, but Naomi stood up from the middle of the crowd where Jevan and Sean were sitting with her. "We fight every time!" Naomi yelled out with her fist in the air. "We stand up for ourselves and we make our voices heard by standing our ground. Running away won't take the problem away. You'll be hiding the rest of your lives and your children's lives if we don't stop it now!"

Just then the doors to the church opened and Deon and Jake walked in. Stella took a breath of relief, though she wasn't sure that anything or anyone could calm this crowd down.

As Deon and Jake walked toward the front of the church, another man in a blue shirt stood and spoke up. "No offense to your husbands, but are they trained in war strategy? I know you can shoot, Jake. I know you were a sniper. But that doesn't mean we know how to win a war."

"I know how to win a fucking war!" boomed a voice from a man so tall and wide he seemed to take up the entire door frame as he entered the church. Behind him was an equally large but older gentleman following him. Both had the same rocking gait to their steps as though the motion kept their large bodies moving forward.

"Who are you?" the man in blue asked.

"I'm Captain Herbert, and this is my father, the admiral. Call me Warren, and he's Abel."

"The first thing we're going to do is combine forces," Abel boomed as loud as his son. Both men were now approaching the platform, joining Stella, Deon, and Jake on the stage. "We need numbers and we need them now. You have families to protect, and so do other outsiders. We're going to band together and win this war. And we *will* win this war."

SATURDAY | JUNE 17, 2073

NAOMI WILCOX

"We thought you were dead!" Naomi proclaimed, throwing her arms around Warren. Warren stepped back and blushed. Naomi guessed he wasn't used to displays of affection. "Oh, stop that," she said as she squeezed him.

"No one can kill us!" Abel replied, his voice filling Naomi and Jake's tiny kitchen.

With Warren, Abel, Jake, Deon, and Stella in the room, Naomi couldn't help but think they may need a bigger house. Warren, Abel, Stella, and Deon sat at the table while Naomi and Jake leaned against the kitchen counter side by side.

"Then who is, I wonder," Deon responded. "Did you know they executed you two on television?"

Warren raised an eyebrow at the question. "I'm not surprised. They'd have to make examples of us to ensure no one else pulled that shit. They probably killed two clones, to be honest. Or prisoners or something like that."

"And how did you know where the Warrens were but the government didn't?" Naomi asked, looking at Jake.

Jake shifted his weight from one foot to another. "Oh,

well, I—"

"Know a guy," Naomi and Jake said together.

Stella smiled as she watched the two of them. Then she turned her gaze to Abel. "They'd kill one of their precious weapons?" she asked.

"They're nothing more than renewable weapons," Abel said. "It takes time for surgery and healing if a dupe gets hurt, about as much as just making a younger and stronger clone. Producing the clones is an industrial assembly line."

"Don't get me started," Naomi said under her breath. Jake elbowed her gently in the side.

"That can't be good for morale," Stella responded, "for older clones to be executed or disappear regularly."

"They don't know. They can't. The main goal is to keep them hoping, like real humans, that they're working toward a better life. They need to believe that to do their job," Abel answered.

"I thought they were programmed to follow commands?" Jake asked.

"They are, but it doesn't hurt to put in a fail-safe as well. They're not only programmed to behave; they get a treat too. Trust me, the last thing the government wants is to imagine a world where the dupes turn against them."

"Then maybe that's what we imagine." Stella stood and walked the length of the room.

"That would be hard to achieve," Warren said.

"I'm not afraid of hard," Stella replied.

"This sounds too big, Stella. We'd have to stop them from attacking us long enough to convince them to start fighting the other direction," Naomi offered.

"They're programmed to fight and programmed to discriminate against us. I agree, this is too big. We need to focus on fighting back. That's our reasonable chance to keep your families safe," Abel said.

"We need to dream of a better world. And we're learning that creating our own better world isn't enough." Stella turned toward them, her eyes wide with determination.

"We need to have a place to raise Jevan." Deon walked over to Stella and reached out to squeeze her hands.

"And what does he do? The same thing we are now? When do we stand up and realize it's up to us to make a better world?" Stella asked Deon, looking into his eyes. Then she turned and looked at the group.

The tension in the room was so thick that Naomi almost couldn't take it. She loved her friend and loved her dedication to the good fight, but she also wanted a place for Sean to grow up. She reached over and grabbed Jake's hand, and she felt him squeeze her hand in response, his way of saying, *It'll be okay*.

After a few minutes of silence, Stella walked toward the door. "I think it's time for bed. Tomorrow we can start recruiting other outsiders and begin our training."

Stella walked tall, but Naomi knew her friend well enough to know she *felt* defeated. They both wanted a different world than this one for their children, but it wasn't possible.

SATURDAY | JUNE 17, 2073

MILES

Living in the training facility with only a few people was almost like being back inside of the tank. The tents were so small that Miles felt confined, but when he left his quarters the base was so big it was like walking through the lab for the first time. Everything was new, foreign. So much had to be learned, and fast. He wanted to sit down and take a moment to put his head between his hands, but he couldn't.

He zigzagged down the pathways between the white tents, thinking about what he'd do when he got more people there. Zac and Leticia remained active. They were both a valuable asset and hard to leave behind, plus both were actively recruiting. Zac was focused on keeping his eyes and ears open to report any news back to his siblings while Leticia was diligently working on altering records. Eventually, Zac would be transitioned to an authoritative position and would be able to share more information. The thing was his eye. Tala and Ramone had figured out how to damage an eye enough to rid it of the two Xs, leaving it blind. As far as the siblings knew, no other dupe had successfully done it before, nor had anyone tried. Dupes were, after all, programmed not to. But would a damaged eye create suspicion? Humans had accidents too, so it wouldn't be that uncommon or far-fetched, but that didn't mean that everyone would easily accept Zac's story about his eye. If Zac got caught, they'd lose him for sure. No doubt they'd execute him—after all, there had been rumors that dupes had been executed for being too injured to work.

He turned right, and the mess hall was before him. They'd not yet received any supplies, but thankfully the first truck was on its way. Andrei was working on the logistics—hacking the military software to alter orders to ship to Miller Base. But it couldn't be rushed and they couldn't add any new vendors, so Andrei had to be careful to only send a little at a time from existing orders or else someone would notice and questions would be asked. The main thing Miles needed to obtain before all went to hell was weapons. Lots of weapons.

Ding.

The sound of a text message. It was Mattie, who was manning the front gate with Asim, informing him that the first shipment had arrived. Miles rushed to the back of the mess hall where the sound of the delivery truck approaching was so loud it reverberated through the kitchen. Miles emerged from the kitchen onto the loading dock and into the bright sunlight.

He wore his military assigned sweats, which meant they were gray. Between his eye and his sweats, there was no way the driver would accept him as authority and Miles hoped the driver wouldn't give a shit and just accept him as a grunt.

Immediately, Mattie and Asim saluted him and stood at attention. Miles felt himself get ruffled. He found that he didn't like to be treated as an authority. He was the same as them—the exact fucking same. He was about to shake his head but realized they were doing it for the driver, to make this operation seem legit.

"It was a long damn way out here. Don't you all have a

provider a little closer? Like in the same state?" the driver said a little loudly while throwing down a case of green beans.

"I can have the administrative staff look into it. I don't know why they'd do that. Must have been an oversight," Miles responded. The truth was, it was easier to use an existing vendor and to keep the order unquestionable than it was to add a new vendor. That would have definitely raised some eyebrows.

"Damn straight it was an oversight. Took me all night to get here."

"As I said, I'll have them look into it." Miles turned his back on the angry man and gave his attention to Mattie and Asim. They were still standing at attention, and that's when he realized he'd never said, *At ease*. It wasn't going to be easy to get used to this shit.

"You two got this?" Miles asked in a loud tone.

"Yes, sir," they both responded.

Should I say at ease now or just walk away? Weren't both options the same thing? He awkwardly wavered in his stance, glanced at the driver, who wasn't paying a bit of attention at all, and then nodded to his two siblings. The edge of Asim's mouth went up just a little, and Miles cut his eyes toward him in response.

Back in his own tent, he was deep in thought about training and strategy when his phone dinged again. *Are the weapons here?* He sure as hell hoped so. They'd be sitting ducks without them.

It wasn't good news; it was Zac, and Zac could only take the chance to communicate when it was pertinent information—life and death information. He looked at the text.

Not long now.

Shit. The cleansing was upon them, and they didn't have much time. He didn't think they were ready. Miles sat back. He didn't have much time. He needed to rush this project, but how? Since he had to try to recruit dupes out of the military without forcing them with a laser or orders, his pace had turned out to be painfully slow. His phone dinged again. This time it was Leticia. He hadn't realized it was a group text. He hoped they were following all precautions in covering their steps.

I've got five hundred troops coming within a month.

Miles rarely responded. When he did, it was always pertaining to strategy. He had to limit his communication to keep them safe even though they knew to delete all evidence of communication.

Five hundred is a big number. That will draw attention.
We need numbers to have a chance.

Yes, they needed numbers. But so far they weren't on the military's radar, and Miles wanted to keep it that way. Since it was an old base, the military hadn't even bothered to fly drones over the Land Between the Lakes. But if five hundred recruits were caught, war would be upon them and soon.

Get weapons now, he texted back.

Miles stood up and walked out of his tent, looking at the sea of white fabric around him, and he realized it was time to stop being so careful. It was time to start making some outside friends.

SUNDAY | JUNE 18, 2073

GIA MORENO

The military houses around Fort Campbell were snug, which was the nicest word Gia could use to describe it. Gia sat on the end of her bed in her split-level home. Looking at her traditional silver watch, which was made from her great-grandfather's pocket watch, she was annoyed it'd only been two minutes. How had they not invented a pregnancy test that took less than five minutes yet? She looked around the room for something to do to pass the time and then huffed. Could she really not just sit for three minutes to find out the results?

She stood up and walked to the door of her bathroom and then stopped. She'd promised herself she wouldn't look until the full five minutes were over, and now there were only two minutes and forty-seven seconds left. She didn't want to see it as negative only for it to turn positive. Did it really work like that though? Would it just appear at the last second? Obviously, that wasn't the way it happened. And if she was pregnant, how far along would she be? Joel had been home from deployment for a few months, and they hadn't missed an opportunity to make up for lost time. She could be anywhere from three weeks to a few months, assuming symptoms would show as soon as that anyway.

She paced her room, walking past and around the bed to a tiny window looking over her neighbor's yard, and then back to the bathroom door again. There was one minute left.

She couldn't take it. She rushed into the bathroom and picked up the pink and white stick. There was a pink happy face on the stick's screen, but the expression didn't match her own. She sat down and let a few tears fall. After a few minutes, she looked at the stick again, and then headed toward the kitchen.

The smell was magnificent. She took in a deep breath. There was definitely curry and garlic and the comforting smell of steaming rice.

"Are you making Indian food?"

"Yes! It's going to be spicy too. I hope you don't mind," Joel responded with a smile.

Her stomach did a flip the moment he said the word *spicy*. She smiled in response.

"No? You don't want spicy?" Joel asked, his happy expression suddenly fallen.

"I didn't say anything. In fact, I smiled!"

"You gave me *the* smile. The I'm-going-along-with-it-but-really-I'm-not-okay smile. If it's not the food, then what is it?"

There was no doubt that Joel loved her, but damn, he was annoying. She couldn't even fake smile without him seeing right through her and pressing her to spill it.

Barry, abandoning his toy toolset, rushed over to Gia, saying, "Mommy! Mommy!" Gia swept him up in her arms and gave him a kiss on his chubby cheek, then walked out of the kitchen into the living room with Joel on her heels.

"Oh no, don't use him as a diversion. What's going on?"

Giving Joel a sideways glance and kissing the side of Barry's head, Gia closed her eyes and a tear fell down her cheek.

Joel touched her shoulder with a gentle rub. "What's

going on?" His voice turned soft, showing her his sensitive side she adored.

"I'm pregnant."

Joel lit up. He wanted a big family more than anything. Another child would be the best news for him while it was the worst for her. Seeing that she didn't smile in response, his face fell again. Guilt began to consume her that she'd made a family with him, married him, even dated such a wonderful man, and therefore pulled him into her twisted world of lies.

"There's more I need to tell you," Gia said. "I've . . ." How could she even begin to tell him everything she'd kept secret from the beginning? She swallowed hard.

Joel gently rubbed both of her shoulders now. "You can tell me anything," he said, which for her, was even more evidence that she didn't deserve him. What if he left her? What if he took Barry? What if he took *both*? But now there was no way out. She couldn't bring another life into this world without Joel truly knowing the danger they were in.

"Do you know what I do?"

Joel stepped back, a look of shock on his face. "Well, we've never really talked about it, but I have an idea."

"I make the clones. I give them the capabilities they need to do their job without emotion."

"Oh." He stood still for a minute, contemplating what she said. "I'm sure that weighs on you. I imagine that's stressful."

"It does. And it is, but the thing is, I did something. I had to take a stand, and I didn't know what else I could do because I couldn't get out of the program." She was talking fast now like she did when she had a lot on her mind. "So, when I was pregnant with Barry, I also made some *special* clones."

Joel released her shoulders. "What do you mean 'special'?"

"I mean, they're different from the other clones. You see, they want me to make the clones non-emotional, and they want them to be followers. I've modified the genome so that they lack the genes that leaders usually have, but there are ten that I didn't do that to. In fact, I gave them very strong leadership skills as well as some other tweaks. I had hoped they would change things, take control, stand up for what's right."

Joel sat down at the kitchen table. There was a burning smell that now filled the house, but neither of them entered the kitchen to check on the food. "You've tried to start a revolution?"

"Yes."

"You've modified the DNA of ten of the clones who may revolt against the United States government?"

"Yes."

"And that's why you're upset that you're pregnant?"

"Yes! I needed you to know. Maybe you and the kids just need to leave before I'm found out. You can take them somewhere safe so when they come for me, you'll be safe."

"Wait, you want me to wait for what, seven months, and then take Barry and a newborn and leave you behind? That's what you're thinking?"

"Yeah, that's it. I don't want you to go through anything."

"That sounds as crazy as modifying the DNA of ten clones to start a war with the United States! Not only did you put all of us in danger, you put all citizens in danger! Gia, I love you, but you're crazy."

"No, this is serious. You don't know what I know . . ." Her words faltered, trying to say everything and nothing at once. ". . . about what the government has done. The things they're capable of."

"You don't think I realize that the government can be ruthless? I work here, too. But *you* didn't think about *our family* when you decided to take your stand!"

"I *did* think about our family! We just didn't *have* a family when I made the embryos. And then it scared the shit out of me when I found out we were having Barry! I'm sorry I've done this—you have no idea how sorry I am. But it's done,

HABITUAL HUMANITY

and I can't hardly sleep or eat for worry and I just want to have a plan for you the kids in case anything happens."

Joel stood up abruptly. "I may not be happy with you right now, and I may not agree with you right now, but you're my wife and I won't leave you, even theoretically in the future." With that, Joel stormed out of the room, passing the pot with heavy smoke billowing out of it.

SUNDAY | JUNE 18, 2073

AUGUST PAXTON

The waiting was the worst. Living in constant readiness for an army of legendary force to appear on the horizon while sitting like a duck, with one rifle in your hands and a handgun in your belt, was daunting—no, terrifying.

But August couldn't say it aloud. If others knew how he felt, they would turn and hide. Not a single person wanted to face what was coming their way, and it would only take a gentle push to send them running to their shelters. To be with their families. To tell their young sons to save themselves and not fight for the Laurel community.

And what was coming for them? A marching, conformed, uncaring battalion of dupes? Or would they also face tanks and helicopters? How much force was the government willing to put behind this cleansing initiative of Laurel?

August looked around. The faces of the old men, grandmothers, the boys with hardly any facial hair poking out from their chins, and everyone else scared him shitless. But he was also proud to be from such a strong community.

Right next to him was Audrey. *You don't dare fight without me*, she'd said. But she was all he had left. The last of their family. And she was supposed to be in their shelter, specifically the underground one, the one he'd built just for her—and for Darius, if he'd ever come out here.

But Darius didn't join August. Instead, he'd stayed in the military and created the very army that now marched toward August and his home. That wasn't the man he'd fallen in love with. *How could he?* What had happened to him? What other secrets had he kept? August would have been by his side and helped. They'd known a long-distance relationship would be hard. *Impossible, more like.*

Despite what Darius did, or what that meant about how much he cared for August, August couldn't lose Audrey. She'd be the last of their family, their last hope of continuing everything their parents had worked so hard for.

He closed his eyes. It was only for a second. Surely, only for a second.

"They're here," Audrey said.

He didn't open his eyes. Had he fallen asleep? Was he dreaming? *More like a nightmare.* This wasn't really about to happen.

"August, the drones," Audrey urged.

Her voice had its usual softness. It had always made him think she was weak and needed protection, but that wasn't the truth. She was stronger than he'd ever imagined. She'd proved that.

He opened his eyes and saw large white drones approaching. The dupes wouldn't be far behind. An hour, a day at most, but not far.

"Please, go to the shelter now. You still have time," August pleaded in a whisper. He didn't want anyone overhearing that he wanted his sister to go hide. What if they also went to hide?

"I need to fight just as you do." She tore her eyes away from the approaching objects to look August in the eye. He saw nothing but pure determination.

"I need someone to survive. I need to know that if I die . . ." He couldn't think about his death now. He'd never been in combat, not like this anyway, but he was sure that thinking of defeat before it even started wouldn't be the best approach.

For the millionth time, he questioned his leadership. He'd never wanted to lead anything like an army. This wasn't the stuff of his dreams, but it had to be done.

"And if you do die, then what do I do? How do I live with that?" Audrey took the rifle strapped across her back and aimed. She took a long breath in, just as August had taught her, and held it. August could feel the release of her breath as though it was his own. It was a long, slow movement. Then there was a loud bang followed by a tiny jolt of her body.

He tensed up and anxiously watched the sky to see what would happen. After a few seconds, one of the drones rolled sideways for a moment and then seemed to try to balance itself. August held his breath. The aircraft wobbled in the air and then nosedived, straight down until it collided with the ground with a loud boom. A huge fireball erupted into the sky.

"That was amazing," a voice from beside them said.

August stood up straight. "And if we do that to all of them, they'll be blind," he yelled to the crowd.

August and his small army took aim.

SUNDAY | JUNE 18, 2073

MILES

Finding communities ended up not being that hard. In fact, the mountains were filled with them. Most were terribly small and didn't have much to offer, not that that was a surprise. But numbers were what mattered, and every little bit counted.

The biggest issue was convincing them to fight with him. After all, a guy with a marked eye and a reputation for violence as a clone probably wasn't the most convincing approach for the outsiders. Most of them had never seen a clone, so if they dared to get close, they pretty much only wanted to stare into his eye. They wanted to know if it hurt to have that modification done to him, and each time, he'd answer honestly that he didn't remember it being done. Unfortunately, even with a soft approach and his candor, most communities wanted very little to do with him. He couldn't blame them, but that didn't stop his frustration.

He'd made it all the way over to North Carolina, which was no small accomplishment. He knew he'd have to head back to camp soon to check in on things. He'd give himself a day here and then head home with only a few hundred extra fighters recruited.

This was so much harder than he'd thought it would be.

He stopped his army vehicle on the side of the road for a much-needed break. When he went to get back into the truck, he saw a pair of eyes staring at him from behind some trees.

"Hello?" Miles called into the dense woods.

The eyes darted behind the tree out of his view.

"I've already seen you, and I'm not going to hurt you." He waited, but there was no answer. However, the person also didn't run away. There was a part of him that he hated, that wanted to roar up and force this person to speak to him. Make them face him and yell in their face, "*Don't judge me! Listen to me!*" Despite the frustration he'd constantly felt during this mission, he knew he couldn't do that.

"I'm not one of them, one of the military. I—"

"You drive their truck! You wear their uniform!" yelled out a female voice.

Most of the outsiders had never seen the uniform or the vehicles. They were all a new design to represent the new army, the Advanced Army. If she'd seen the uniform and vehicle before, she hadn't been here very long. Miles wasn't sure that honesty was the best policy with this girl, but he had no choice, since she'd already called him out. "Yeah, you're right. I stole them from them."

"Likely story."

"A true one. Look." Miles took out his guns and his knives and laid them in front of the black military Jeep and then re-approached the edge of the forest, more than ten feet away from where he'd laid the weapons down. "I put down my weapons!"

"That's not enough."

"What else can I do?"

"Nothing. I've been up against your kind before." Her voice came from further to the north now.

"I see." His assumption had been right. He was fascinated and wanted to know more. "Were you evicted during the cleansing?"

"Evicted, eradicated, removed—there are multiple words I could use." The sound of her voice moved again.

"So, you were in New York?"

"Obviously."

"And were those soldiers like I am now?"

She didn't answer.

"They're coming here, to the outside, to complete the cleansing." He waited, but she gave no response. Deciding he was wasting his time, he gave up, believing he'd lost all chances of connecting with her. He started to turn back toward his Jeep when he saw that his weapons were gone. He froze. How could he be that stupid?

"That was a good move," he called out, holding his arms out and turning in a slow circle. "Are you going to kill me now?"

"That's not in me."

There was something in the way she said it that let him know it was true. So far, his profile of her was a woman, evicted from New York during the cleansing, who was smart and fast, but also forgiving. He liked her.

"I wish I could say the same." He liked that she was being transparent, and perhaps it would work to play the same card.

"You're not made that way." The voice was almost next to him.

He turned to see a young woman emerging from the forest, aiming his own gun at him. She had wild black hair with striking blue eyes. "But I'm not going to hurt you," he responded.

"What are you doing here?" She kept her distance at five feet from him.

"I'm looking to recruit people to fight back."

She furled her eyebrows. "What?"

"I have a group of soldiers willing to fight with you. We're trained, we want to fight back, and we'll do it for both your freedom and ours. We can work together." He'd said

HABITUAL HUMANITY

the words so much over the past few days, they flowed out of him like a powerful waterfall. If he'd wanted to say it any other way, he wouldn't have had the choice. The power of the words was too strong, rising up from his will through his vocal cords and taking control.

"Clones want to fight for the freedom of clones *and* outsiders?"

"We're different. It's hard to believe, but we are. And we can help convert other clones to be like us."

"You're asking for a lot of trust. How would we know that this isn't a ploy?"

"It's not. If it was, we'd have already stormed in and taken my weapons back."

"So you're asking me to fight *with* you?"

"Is it just you?"

She paused. "Yes, it's just me."

He smiled. That was the first lie she'd told him. "The army is coming. If you want protection, we'll protect you."

"And in return, I have to fight with you."

"Yes." He left his answer simple because it was a simple truth. There were no surprises in this agreement.

"It will take time for me to consider."

"I've got almost a thousand troops to help in your fight against the Advanced Army. Please drop my weapons and consider my offer. I'll come back tomorrow and wait for you here for your answer."

Cautiously, she took a few steps back and then placed his weapons on the ground. Then she sprinted away into the woods like a deer.

The next day, Miles arrived early on purpose, not wanting to miss her, and sat on the hood of his Jeep without any weapons. He was in the exact same spot, which he'd marked by chalk on the ground the day before. He came prepared to sit a while, as he was willing to guess from her personality that she'd make him wait. That thought brought up feelings he didn't expect.

She didn't make him wait long. Only forty minutes after

the time he'd given her, a troop of cars came down the road toward him. He knew she'd lied when she'd said she was alone, but he hadn't guessed she had that much force behind her. There were at least five cars approaching him, and some were armed military vehicles of an older variety of his own, back when they painted them camouflage rather than the flat black of his Jeep. Miles was even more impressed; this girl had much more to her than he'd ever guessed. Now, he realized, she'd been here before him, watching him, making sure he was alone. And, he guessed, the numbers that he brought dictated several factors, like whether or not they even showed up and how many they brought with them. He was alone and they brought five vehicles. Maybe there was one person in several of those vehicles, but it was still a good show of muscle. If he'd brought five people, or five vehicles, then would they have brought fifteen? He liked this group.

The young woman wasn't the one that got out of the first vehicle. It was a middle-aged black man.

"Thank you for coming," Miles said in greeting. He slid off the front of his Jeep and took a few steps toward the man, who didn't recoil or aim his gun in response. He was wearing the older style military uniform. "Have you thought about my offer?"

"I've come to hear the offer for myself."

"It's pretty simple. I'll bring my army to join yours in a fight against the Advanced Army, if you help us fight them in return."

"So, it's true, you're a clone, banding together with other clones, to fight the United States Army?"

"That's right."

The man took a deep breath and looked around. "You're the only one here?"

"Yeah, I'm looking for allies."

"Where's your base?"

Miles hesitated before answering, since giving up too much information could be dangerous. But he knew he needed this group to trust him, so he took a chance. "The

HABITUAL HUMANITY

Land Between the Lakes in Tennessee."

"That's not close to here," the man responded, not hiding his surprise.

"No, I've been all over trying to build our army. We have weapons, training, and gumption. We need numbers. We can teach you anything you need to know."

The man glanced over his shoulder and nodded.

This time two white men got out of the Jeep, also dressed in old military uniforms. One was a tall thick man, and the other was about Miles' size.

"I think we're good on the training," roared the larger man.

Miles liked this group more and more—a group of trained soldiers already having escaped from the system themselves. He needed their help. They needed his help. He had to find a way to convince them. Soldier to soldier, there had to be a way. "We're coming from the inside, with inside knowledge and strategy. We know how to beat them. Will you join us?"

"It's not our place to decide," replied the other white man.

"I can tell you're a group that knows how it's going to go down. And I can tell you know you need my help to survive."

"I'm not saying we do or don't," replied the black man.

"Who do I need to convince?" Miles asked.

"It's more complicated than convincing one person. But—" he glanced at the other two men "—next, you need to talk to Stella, my wife." The man turned toward one of his comrades and said, "Jake, pat him down."

Miles automatically put his hands behind his head and spread his legs. Jake walked over and patted down Miles' body. Finding no weapons, he yelled, "Clear." If they were surprised, they didn't show it.

"You'll leave your Jeep here," the large white man said.

"No problem," Miles replied. He then followed Jake and willingly got into the back of the first vehicle, an old SUV he didn't recognize as a modern brand. When all the men were also inside, Miles said, "Don't knock me out; just put a bag over my head."

"Deal. My name is Deon. This is Warren." Deon nodded to the large white man that'd gotten into the front passenger side. "And that's Jake."

"I'm Miles."

Deon nodded and Jake put a black bag over Miles' head.

MONDAY | JUNE 19, 2073

STELLA HOPKINS

There was no way to set expectations for meeting a stranger. So many had come through, and just as many had provided nothing more than disappointments. Meeting with other off-the-grid communities was common, and often without success of an agreement of any kind. Fines Creek had a few communities to trade with but had little to no success in finding anyone to band together and fight. Not that she blamed them. Even with their military training, she was terrified of the massive unit of soldiers with a collective sociopathic mind that was hunting them.

Soldiers and a way to fight back were what this *clone* was offering. A thousand, to be exact, to help their community, but she didn't buy it. The fact that she was judging him before even meeting him sent a jolt of disgust through her. Did that make her just like those that judged her for being black or a woman? Or whatever it was that they decided not to like about her?

No, she reminded herself. *That's not it. A clone is a completely different species altogether. Clones were modified to be dangerous, and that did make them different.*

But what if? What if it were possible that they could change? She shook her head. *No, they can't. This isn't going to work, even if he claims to have numbers.*

"Hi," said a soft voice Stella had grown to love as much as her own son's.

She turned to see Ocean standing in the doorway. "Hello."

"He'll be here soon," Ocean said and her eyes brightened.

Did Ocean like this man she'd met only yesterday? Within the community, there weren't many Ocean's age. This man would be one of the few within her age group she'd met since Arnav.

"I don't know. They probably won't trust him enough to bring him," Stella said, looking Ocean in the eye. She hoped her motherly vibe of *don't get your hopes up* and *please no, not this boy* came across loud and clear.

"They will. He's the ally we need." Ocean turned away, leaving Stella feeling even more hopeless. She wished she was this girl's mother. She wished she'd had her since a baby and had every right to tell her not to get her hopes up, not to care about this man. After all, there were truly bigger and more pertinent things for Ocean to concern herself with.

She had no idea how long she'd been lost in thought, but the sound of Ocean's voice saying, "They're here," brought her out of her concentration.

They actually brought him to my house? Stella had to see for herself, so she stood and approached the window and looked out with Ocean by her side.

Deon parked the SUV and Stella watched him, Jake, and Warren guide a man with a black hood over his head out of the back seat.

A moment later, the men were guiding the mysterious man inside the house that Stella had even more reason to send away. Stella and Ocean sat on the couch as Deon guided the man to an armchair. Jake and Warren stood to one side while Deon squatted in front of the clone.

"I'm going to take your hood off. If you do anything, I'll kill you. If you say anything rude, I'll hit you," Deon said.

"Got it." The voice that emerged from under the hood sounded like a tenor from a choir, much too beautiful and disturbingly controlled.

"I want to be sure you got it. This is my wife, and I will protect her with my life." Stella recognized the tense tone that Deon was using. It was one she'd only heard a few times, and each time, it was because he was protecting either Jevan or her.

Could that hooded individual understand marriage? Family? He didn't grow up with a family, didn't watch his parents hold hands, kiss, or even fight. Were clones allowed to marry? Did they have any capability of love if they'd been modified to hate? She had so many questions and too many reasons to want this man out of her house.

The clone nodded. "I will never harm her."

Deon looked at her with a question in his eyes. She wanted to ask if he was crazy. She wanted to say that he'd made a very bad choice. But she trusted Deon and knew he'd never put her in harm's way. She also trusted Jake and Warren, and they'd also chosen to trust this clone. She felt her heart beating against her ribcage and, if she didn't know better, would even proclaim her blood pressure was rising. She nodded her head at Deon.

Deon nodded in return and slipped off the hood from the man's head in one movement.

The dupe had a short haircut and a full beard. When he smiled, it lit up his entire face and his eyes wrinkled at the edges. As normal and friendly as the rest of his face was, she was shocked and scared at the sight of the black and white Xs embedded into his right iris. "Hello, I'm Miles." He kept his hands in his lap. *Smart move.*

"I'm Stella," she replied.

"Are you in charge of the community?"

"I am the voice."

Miles smiled and nodded.

HABITUAL HUMANITY

"How has it come to be that a clone is looking to fight against clones?"

"I am not fighting *against* clones but *for* my own kind."

Stella allowed the silence to fill the room as she waited for him to continue.

"Most dupes, on what we call our awakening day, wake in a large warehouse in long rows of other clones. But not me. I woke on a metal bed, alone in a room. A woman came to see me, a doctor. I've come to think of her as Mother. She confided in me that she didn't trust those she worked for and that she'd made me to be different."

Stella had often wondered what it would be like to be a doctor there and what their role actually was. How much did they know? People believed that doctors were supposed to be caring individuals, but that wasn't always reality. Some doctors had a Mr. Hyde personality. Others were Frankensteins. But it was possible there were good doctors in awful situations who either didn't know the implications of their work or who, quite possibly, were forced to do what they did. From what he'd just shared, it sounded as though they were quite possibly forced. Stella leaned forward and urged him to continue. "Go on."

"Mother told me I was one of few that she'd made. Currently, I have met eight of my siblings, four sisters and four brothers."

"She made five boys and four girls?" Ocean asked.

Miles looked directly at Ocean, and for a moment, Stella forgot her fascination with his story. Internally, she switched into mother mode and didn't want this man talking to Ocean at all. Against her aching heart and instinct, she allowed him to answer Ocean's question.

"I believe I have another sister, and I'm still looking for her." Turning his attention back to Stella, he said, "That's how it is that a dupe is sitting here before you both offering and asking for help. You need to fight back in order to remain in control of your land and your life, and we need to fight for our freedom."

"Fighting back is never easy. It's been tried many times, and look at us now," Stella replied.

"But I must fight for my people. I believe I'm programmed to do so, so I have no choice." His smile remained, but the light in his eyes faltered.

"Just like the other clones?"

He nodded. "But not in the same way."

Warren stepped forward. "To be clear, you want us to trust about a thousand dupes to enter our community and believe they won't kill us on your word?"

"I understand the situation you're in. It's not an easy easy decision—but I ask you, what chance do you have without us?."

"How did you manage to convert clones?" Warren asked.

"We're working on rehabilitating them to fight for us. What we really need is a two-photon laser…" Before he finished, Abel interrupted him.

"The ones used to program the dupes their orders?"

"Those exactly. But we don't want to program them to fight, we want to erase their orders and give them the opportunity to choose."

"That could have unexpected ramifications," Jake added.

Stella looked Miles directly in his strange, marked eye. "Even if I'm willing to fight by your side, even if I trust you, God forbid even if I start to like you, how could I open my community up to an army of clones after announcing to them that's exactly who is going to kill them?"

"That's the part I leave up to you as their voice," Miles replied.

Stella sat back and nodded toward Deon. She'd had enough of this meeting, and the men could question him more as they drove him back.

"It's time to go," Deon said to Miles.

A moment of surprise flashed across Miles' face, but he responded, "Yes, sir." He waited for Jake to put the black bag over his head. Within minutes, they were gone, leaving Stella and Ocean alone again.

HABITUAL HUMANITY

"He has an army," Ocean said as she grabbed Stella's hands. Ocean was soft, young, and way too trusting.

"He's a clone." Stella stood up and walked into the kitchen to heat water for tea. She had a beautiful jasmine plant in the yard, and it had become one of her favorite habits to steep the jasmine with tea leaves.

"He's not like the others," Ocean replied, hot on Stella's heels.

Girl, if you only knew how many women have said that before you.
"I don't think it's a good idea," Stella said as she filled a kettle with water.

"But it's not your choice."

Stella quickly turned to look Ocean in the eye. Ocean had never talked back to her like that before, never defied her. "Excuse me?"

Ocean's blue eyes were both scared and angry. "You're our voice, but you're not supposed to decide for us. *We* get to decide."

Stella turned away, taking the kettle to the stove and putting it down with a loud clang. She stood there for a moment while all of her fears were pushed to the side by Ocean's words. "You're right. That's not who I am or who I want to be, nor the type of community we'd hoped to build. It's their families, their own lives. And it's their choice."

MONDAY | JUNE 19, 2073

AUGUST PAXTON

The Laurel community had taken out all the drones. The cheers from their miniature army was a beautiful sound. Then they waited for what seemed like ages as the darkness rolled in on a night so cloudy that no stars appeared. Some kept watch while others slept as best they could leaning against a shaky, wooden bunker they'd built in haste, holding whatever weapon they had against their chest, trying to be ready even in their slumber. That's when, in the quiet of a morning fog, a voice rang out from among them.

"THEY'RE HERE!"

August turned and saw, on the horizon cresting a hill, shadows of a unit that marched unlike any he'd ever seen. There were dozens of vehicles and thousands of soldiers marching on foot. If the military could spare this many to march on Laurel, then how giant was the military of these clones?

August looked back at his own. A couple hundred men, only a dozen horses, and a few trucks.

He didn't even want to compare the weapons.

HABITUAL HUMANITY

He wouldn't blame any of his own if they ran.

No one did.

He thought about commanding that they should, in fact, run away. Save themselves, save their families. Go and hide. But was there anywhere to hide from something like this?

"TAKE YOUR PLACES!" August yelled.

The Laurel army, if it could even be called an army, got down into their bunkers and took the safety off their guns, pointing their weapons toward the enemy.

August walked through the bunker, hitting everyone on the backs. "They may have the numbers, but we have something worth fighting for. We have family, they don't. We have land, they don't. They have no reason to fight, but we do! Our families have lived here for a thousand years, and it will stay that way for a thousand more! We've already taken out their eyes! We have the advantage! We will win!"

He almost believed his words himself.

His neighbors, childhood friends, and extended community yelled and cheered in response. August took his place in the bunker, aiming his rifle, ready to die.

TUESDAY | JUNE 20, 2073

DARIUS JONES

It had been difficult to get information about where the units were and what they'd accomplished. Darius' job was only to create them, after all; beyond that, it really wasn't any of his business. He hadn't heard from August, and he'd tried. He'd left messages apologizing, telling him he loved him. Telling him he was ready to join him. Ready to give up on this dream that had done nothing more than become a living nightmare. But on his end, the satellite phone never rang, never showed a missed call, and never offered a voicemail.

It was the biggest fight he and August had ever been in, and it was also the only time he'd ever lied to August. Would August forgive him? Would he eventually call him back? At first, he'd been certain he would, but he hadn't. And now he couldn't help but wonder. More than that, he wondered where the military was and what August was living through. That thought was too much. He'd rather August not call him back because he was angry, not because of war.

He stared at the phone. Should he call again? Or should he give August more time? There was a giant army of clones marching toward his boyfriend, so of course he should call.

He sat on the edge of his bed and pressed the number. The phone began to ring. No answer yet, and August always answered right away, so Darius knew he wasn't going to answer. But what if he was just busy? After two rings, the chances were even lower. If it rang a fourth time, he'd hang up. It wasn't worth leaving another voicemail.

It didn't ring again. His heart thudded within his chest. In one second, he'd hear August's caring, beautiful voice. Everything was going to be okay and he could tell him that he'd leave this terrible place, that nothing was more important than being together. He was freed from that agreement with the military when the clones became public knowledge.

But it wasn't August's voice. It was a woman's. "Hello?"

Darius wasn't sure what to say. These phones were secret, and no one else ever used them.

"Is this Darius?" the woman asked.

It was Audrey, August's sister. What was she doing answering his phone? Darius' voice caught in his throat when he said, "Yes, this is Darius. Is August there?" There wasn't time for formal politeness when he was worried about his partner. The only thing that mattered was August. After that, he could talk to Audrey and properly introduce himself.

There was a pause and Darius felt relief that August was coming to the phone. But he didn't come to the phone. Instead, the next sound Darius heard was Audrey crying. "They're here, thousands of them."

The black hole grew.

"August led the rebellion, but our numbers were too small," Audrey said between sniffles.

The black hole took over Darius' entire vision. He was no longer in his bedroom, but in a vast universe without planets or suns; there was no end to the encompassing darkness.

"August fought as long as he could, but he . . ." Her sobs increased such that she couldn't speak.

"Is he dead?" Darius asked.

HABITUAL HUMANITY

In a whisper, Audrey replied, "Yes."

TUESDAY | JUNE 20, 2073

MILES

"So, they'll join us?" Mattie asked.

"We will fight with them and help them. We'll show them the vision we're fighting for, and yes, they'll fight with us," Miles responded.

"That doesn't sound promising enough. We can't go on the line for just anyone," Asim replied.

"Agreed, but they're not just anyone. They're the strongest, most coordinated group we've come across. We need them," Miles said.

"Do they know the full extent of our plans?" Mattie asked.

"It wasn't the time. But, this is how we make allies." Miles got up and walked out of Mattie's tent. Their reaction had dampened his enthusiasm just a bit. These things were not simple, never straight-forward, and it wasn't easy to trust. In fact, Miles couldn't think of a more complicated and unpredictable time to live. War had to be hardest, second or equal to only pandemics.

Miles knew if Fines Creek wanted to survive, they had no other choice, whether they trusted him and his clones or not.

And he felt sure some of them would join in his endeavor to change things permanently. They'd help him overthrow the United States government, and he'd need them to help put everything back together again.

The other recruits had also found some communities, much smaller in numbers, and they needed them all. That was the funny thing about numbers, Miles told them; they added up.

He was walking through the center of the personal tents area when he saw a woman emerge from one of the pathways. He froze in place, stunned. This woman had the long brown hair, the tiny body, the quick mannerisms, but she was wearing the gray sweats of a dupe. There was no way she could possibly be here. If a high-ranking official had come here, the Advanced Army would have followed. They would have swarmed in and killed everyone.

She turned down a side path through the jungle of tents, drying laundry, and soldiers playing cards.

"Hey Gianna, wanna play a game?"

"No thanks, Cole," she replied. She'd turned just slightly when she said it, and Miles got a good view of her face.

It had to be her. *Mother.*

Miles felt like a lost dog that'd finally found his way home. He wanted her to hug him. Wanted her to say he was on the right track and was doing well. Some form of love. *Is this what it felt like to be a child? Is this why the ache for her never went away?*

But there was no way it was her; it was impossible for it to be true.

When Miles walked by, the soldiers playing cards stood and saluted him. He returned the salute and nodded, trying not to seem as though he was following someone. What would he do if she saw him? Or even speak to him? What would he say? Would he yell at her and ask her why? Why did she give him this burden?

After a few more minutes, she ducked into a tent.

He quickly turned down another path and weaved in and

HABITUAL HUMANITY

out between several tents until, finally, he found his own and sat down on his cot deliberating the information he'd just observed. Everything about her pointed to Mother, but there was no way. It didn't make sense that she'd either be missing or had gone AWOL without them knowing. And he wouldn't accept that she was a potential spy. They'd been so careful to ensure they couldn't be traced.

Even the recruits didn't know. They were sent on a multi-stop journey, never knowing the eventual destination, and their papers were fake. And then, frankly, they were kind of trapped. Though at this time, no one had tried to leave—yet. So, if the only ones that knew of this base were his siblings, and the only others that had come here were the recruits, then . . . she's a recruit. Mother must have cloned herself.

That's my sister. That was why they'd never found her—Mother had to have sent Gianna away from the base immediately, or else those on the base would have recognized her dupe. Gianna probably didn't know that she was different, that she was the clone of a leading doctor in the program. Or that she had a family.

TUESDAY | JUNE 20, 2073

DARIUS JONES

Darius looked down at the phone. It was his only link to August, but August wasn't there. The plastic unfeeling thing mocked him. This link to the one person he loved and who had loved him no matter what wasn't a link at all. It was a black hole, swallowing his hand. It had a shrieking laugh as it grew and began to eat him alive.

He threw it down. It was nothing now. He was nothing now. How did it turn out like this?

What could he do? It was 7:30 am, and he had fifteen minutes without August on the other line to chat away about cows, or mending fences, or his sister showing up out of the blue. Fifteen minutes of emptiness.

He stood in the kitchen, but he didn't know how he got there. What could he do? *Make eggs.* He always made eggs in the morning. The egg carton was buttercup yellow and cold to the touch. He'd always imagined that he'd make eggs for August one day before he ran out into the field. And Darius would have a practice in Laurel where he actually helped people. *Helped* people, not manufactured them. No

HABITUAL HUMANITY

modifications for a malevolent purpose. *Will I ever help anyone or just hurt them?*

The cracking sound of the eggs echoed in his ears. It was so silent in his apartment. Did he really live like this? Did the sound of cooking eggs fill a room? His heart? His soul? *No, August did that.*

How could he live with this emptiness? Maybe that wasn't the right question. Why should he live? What was there to live for?

He threw the scrambled eggs into the trash and threw the pan into the sink. The resulting clanging was so loud, it hurt his ears. He covered them with his hands. *This isn't living.*

It was 7:45 am. He gathered his things and walked outside. Now what? Did he wait the ten minutes for Hector and Mollie? No, the black hole would swallow him, and it would swallow him with that shrieking laugh. He walked.

The dupes were already up and training, as always. The sounds of the commands while the men ran offered the normalcy Darius sought, but it didn't console him. Routine wasn't going to be enough today. Would it ever be again? Would he ever be the same again? *No, I am not going to be the same without August.* If he couldn't be okay, then what was he? And what was left for him?

Somehow, he was standing in front of the building where the practice was. How long had he worked here? Had that much time truly passed since August left the military? How could he let any of this happen? It was all his fault.

"Alaine, Darius Jones reporting for duty."

"Thank you, Darius. You may enter."

The door clicked open. Within minutes, he was in the practice, but he didn't remember walking through the door. Was his morning really happening or was all this some surreal dream? Part true and part not? Could he choose to go back in time and change it all? Even if they had the power of time, would that be possible? And if it weren't possible, did that mean no one ever actually had any choice, that the power of choice was all an illusion?

"Darius, are you okay? Your color is off," Gia said, approaching him.

"What?" Darius asked.

"I've said hello several times and you didn't answer. You look like hell."

"I'm sorry, I didn't hear you. I'm fine." He added a smile for effect.

"I don't believe you for a second. Go into the first exam room." Gia pulled two blue plastic gloves from a box marked XS.

"No, really, I'm fine."

"No, really, you're not. I've never seen you like this. We're not close friends, I get that, but I know you better than that."

Maybe he should tell her. They'd kept secrets for one another; maybe that did constitute as a close friend or perhaps just human kindness? "August . . ." Darius started, but then his voice caught.

Gia knew about August; it was part of Darius' file that he was close to the seaman that'd gone AWOL and never found. But when she had the apartment next to his, she'd also figured out that's who Darius had talked to on the phone. She was the only one who knew they still had a relationship. When Darius didn't continue, her eyebrows furled. "What about August?"

"August . . ." Darius tried to start again. But if he said it, would that make it true? Could he say it? "The *Cleansing*." It was all he could get out.

Gia's eyes grew wide. "Is he okay?"

Darius shook his head.

"Is he . . . gone?"

Unable to say it, Darius nodded, but even that simple movement was enough to make it real. The grief overtook him, starting in his heart and quickly engulfing his body like a wildfire. His shoulders shook and he cried out. Doubling over, his mouth opened in a silent scream, and his drool collected on the floor.

"I'm so sorry. I'm so sorry." Gia kept repeating the words. He felt her arms wrap around him and then gently pull him to the back office. She stayed with him and rubbed his back until his sobs became a soft cry.

"They killed him," Darius said when he could catch his breath again. Then he looked her directly into her eyes. "We killed him."

THURSDAY | JUNE 22, 2073

STELLA HOPKINS

She wasn't sure, but the waiting had to be the worst part. No, knowing her family was in danger while the attack happened would certainly be worse. But now, the waiting was beating in her head like a drum. *Are they here? It is time? Are they here? It is time?*

Somewhere there was an army in formation marching toward her, the people she loved, and the community she'd give anything for. The thought was terrifying. Had they made the right decision to band together with clones? Would they turn on them once the army arrived and massacre them? She stood in the zone dedicated for the wounded. Though part of her felt she should be fighting, she knew that wasn't a talent she possessed. Her talent was healing, not hurting.

She looked over at Jevan, her beautiful son.

He nodded at her and said, "Mom, it's okay. Don't worry."

Oh, if such things were true. In the past few years while training him in medicine, never once had she pictured him working on wounded soldiers in a battlefield. This isn't what she wanted for her son, nor Ocean. Stella had tried to force

HABITUAL HUMANITY

Ocean into the bunker with the children, but she'd refused. Not only had she refused, but she wanted to be with Miles' troop. Stella's heart ached in worry for the girl. Then her thoughts rushed to Deon, the man she envisioned growing old with. As many times as they'd said *I'll see you later* while wondering if it'd be the last time, it never got easier. They refused to ever say goodbye. She trusted Deon's decisions more than any other. And then Naomi and Jake, their best friends. They were standing on the front lines, ready for battle. Stella knew that couldn't be easy for Jake, knowing Naomi was there. He'd never had that concern before, but Naomi couldn't stand down while everyone else fought. Only Sean was in the bunker, his body too weak for fighting. Had they trained enough? Could they possibly win? They'd all heard the stories about other communities that were easily wiped out.

Her radio blasted into life. "Visual in the south," said Warren's voice.

Abel had thought the south was the most likely approach for the Advanced Army. There wasn't a good approach to Fines Creek, being so deep in the mountains. The trees and elevation gave them an advantage as well as knowing the land so well, whereas it was all new territory for the Advanced Army.

"Visual in the east," said Miles' voice.

That was the other option they'd considered, that the army might try a boxing maneuver by forcing an attack on all sides. Abel taught them to be prepared for anything, teaching as many strategies as he thought possible for their circumstance.

"They may have the numbers, but we'll have a plan," Abel had said so many times his words had entered her dreams more than once.

"Hold," came Warren's voice. They already knew he'd make them wait past the point of comfortability; the man knew what he was doing.

Miles and Warren were using the only infrared sensors

HABITUAL HUMANITY

they had and all Stella could do was imagine what they saw. Did they see a few soldiers manuerving slowly through the thick forest like scouts? Or did they see so many inching forward it sent fear down their spine?

"Hold," came Warren's voice again, reassuring their soldiers.

Waiting wasn't the worst. Knowing danger was upon them and there was nothing she could do was the worst. Picturing her husband on the front line, though she'd done it before, was the worst. Picturing everyone she knew right now in harm's way was the worst. She closed her eyes, trying hard not to see her worst fears come true. *As long as our children are okay in the end.*

"FIRE!" Warren rang through the radios. Stella jumped at the command. Then the sound of gunshots in the distance rang through the trees. It became louder and louder and then engines roared to life. Tears fell down her face.

FRIDAY | JUNE 23, 2073

STELLA HOPKINS

The field was full of injured soldiers. Stella and Jevan were in the weeds, yelling out commands to those that had volunteered to help them despite barely having any training. It had been difficult to accept before today that she and her son were the most qualified individuals to save the lives of those trying to save them. But now, running from one wounded soldier to the next and trying to help them all, there was no time to reflect on who she could have trained, the school she should have started, or any other of the multitude of ideas that would have better prepared them for this day.

It was then that she looked over and saw Jevan standing like a statue, staring at a soldier as though he'd never seen blood before. What could it be that had her son so stunned?

The soldier she was working on would live. He had broken ribs but no major damage to organs. She rushed over to Jevan's side and caught her breath. It was Deon, unconscious, shot, and bleeding.

She looked over at one of their volunteers. "Take him!" she yelled, pointing toward Jevan. He shouldn't see his father

HABITUAL HUMANITY

like this. She ripped open Deon's uniform. He'd been shot four times. Two of the shots had gone straight through, and he was losing a lot of blood. The other two could be lodged within major organs.

He wasn't going to make it.

Tears ran down her face, but she couldn't think like that now. She had to save him.

"SCALPEL!" She had to get the bullets out.

She cut him open, which meant he was losing more blood.

"GET A TRANSFUSION!"

As a doctor, she knew he was going to die. She knew the precious blood could save someone else's life that would have a chance, but this was her husband. The father of her son. They needed him. She had to do this.

The volunteer started the transfusion as Stella got the first bullet out. It was only in a muscle; it would be okay. But where was the other?

"STAY WITH ME, DEON! DO YOU HEAR ME?"

There was no response. She found the other bullet in his heart, which was barely beating. She knew she didn't have long.

"YOU CAN'T DO THIS!"

He didn't respond.

She clamped her hands around his face. His blood was everywhere.

"STAY WITH ME!"

His heart stopped beating. She exploded in tears. She couldn't do this. She couldn't do this anymore. She collapsed on the ground next to Deon and cried into his shoulder as she had many times before, but this time, his arm didn't wrap around her.

Something was shaking her, but she didn't want to look up. She couldn't get up. There was nothing left within her. But then a pair of hands forced her to look. She saw one of the volunteers screaming at her with wide eyes and blood prints on her face. She was frantic and asking for help. Stella sat up and then stood up and took in the gruesome scene around her. More soldiers were wounded. No, not soldiers. They were neighbors, friends. Stella took a step and looked upon a neighbor trying to save another, so Stella barked out orders. He would be saved. She approached another citizen and yelled at a volunteer to come help, telling him what needed to be done. She'd be saved too.

Her heart couldn't move, but her feet did. Her brain did what it always did: looked for a solution. Her hands did what they always did: they healed. And then Jevan approached her and it all came crashing down again.

"Jevan?" she tried to say it with a strong, comforting motherly tone, but it came out as a question instead. It was a question she was really asking herself. *Are you ready to hear the news? How are you going to take it? How will we make it through this day?*

What he said in response wasn't what she expected. It was the same thing she'd just asked him. "Mom?"

She knew he had more bad news.

"It's Naomi," he said, his voice low and his eyes shiny from tears.

FRIDAY | JUNE 23, 2073

DARIUS JONES

Darius lay in a warm bath in his tiny white bathroom. Showers were more of his style, and now he knew for a fact that his bath was indeed too small for him. His knees poked out of the water and his shoulders touched both sides of the tub.

What was appropriate to do now? Was this his goodbye to August? Should he say a few words? He supposed that all depended on whether or not he believed in God, or more specifically, an afterlife. If he did, then that made sense. But he didn't, so really anything he did was for himself and not for August, making it nothing more than a selfish gesture.

But was that so bad, to be selfish during a time when he'd lost the man he loved? Didn't he deserve time to grieve? Time to say goodbye? He'd done everything else so very wrong, certainly he could get this one thing right.

Tears streamed down his face. He stifled his cries, but then remembered that no one could hear him anyway. He could scream bloody murder and not a soul would hear him from the empty apartments that surrounded his own. That thought led to the mental image that it would be Mollie or

HABITUAL HUMANITY

Hector that came in on Monday morning, wondering why he wasn't standing in his usual spot to greet them. Could he do that to them? Then he let it go, crying like a scared child until he was cried out and the water had gone lukewarm.

He held his breath and picked up a razor blade he'd set on the edge of the tub. His hand shook violently, and he released his breath in a rush that was so forceful, the action shook his entire body. He put the razor blade down. He couldn't do it while he was so unstable. Closing his eyes, he waited a few moments before picking up the blade again. Again, his hand shook violently.

Is this what it was like for my mother?

His head fell back against the tub with a thud and he blinked at the ceiling, not seeing nor unseeing. Maybe it got easier over time. Maybe one day he'd pick up the razor and just cut his wrist, unfeeling. Or perhaps it would finally bring him happiness.

He heard a knock at the door, which made him jump. Getting out of the tub, he began to shiver. He hadn't even realized how cold the water had become. It seemed strange to go through the motion of putting on a robe, as though life was all right, things like answering the door actually mattered, and that it was good to see people.

It wasn't acceptable to think like that. August was gone. Life would never be all right again, and it wasn't okay to think or act as though it was.

Opening the door a crack, he was embarrassed to see Mollie standing there. He pulled at his robe so that the soft thick fabric covered his chest completely. He tried to look her in the eye, but instead kept dropping his gaze off to the side, not being used to feeling so indisposed in front of someone.

"Oh, hi!" she said as she tried to look away. "I didn't mean to interrupt."

"No, I was getting out of the bath. I should have put on something else. I was not sure if the matter was urgent." In reality, he hadn't put any thought into it. He'd simply gone through the motions without any concern about who was knocking at the door. But to sound convincing, he added a small smile and tried to look at her directly once again.

"Not urgent, just movie night. Hector and I wanted to invite you."

Movie night? What a ridiculous notion. Does she know the soldiers we manufactured are killing innocent people? Is there anything about me that hints the love of my life has just been taken from me? And that it's all our fault? How can we just watch a movie? "That sounds nice. What time?"

"Really? Oh, dinner is at seven, sort of. We kind of lose track of time sometimes, but we'll have food. And then we'll start the movie around eight." Mollie was still not looking him in the eye. He couldn't blame her. He'd never been so embarrassed.

"I will see you and Hector at seven."

"Great! See you then," Mollie said, her eyes brightening. She turned to walk away.

Darius never liked to include himself in the affairs of others, but he felt very much removed from his usual self at this time, and so words came out of his mouth that he couldn't quite explain if he had to. "Mollie?"

She turned, eyebrows raised.

"I hope you give Hector a chance."

"What do you mean?" She'd cocked her head to the side and her eyebrows furled. He'd certainly caught her off guard.

"I mean, I could be wrong, but from my observations, he cares for you. And no one should miss an opportunity to love someone, to spend time with them." It took everything he had to stop the tears as he said it.

Mollie shifted her gaze from Darius to the wall and back to Darius again.

"Again, I could be wrong. I'll never mention it again," Darius added, feeling even more embarrassed and out of place.

Mollie cocked her head to the side just a little. "You really think he likes me?"

Darius smiled, but in a flash, it was gone. "I do."

Mollie smiled in return. "See you later!" she said before she walked away.

Darius wasn't sure, but he thought he saw a skip in her step. For a moment, that made everything good. Maybe, he'd done something to help someone else not make the same mistake he did, but as he turned back into his apartment, the black hole was waiting to swallow him yet again.

FRIDAY | JUNE 23, 2073

MILES

The death and destruction weren't a shock. Miles had been trained for this. But to watch his comrades die in battle because he'd asked them to tormented him in a way he didn't expect. Did this all add up to being enough? Was it worth it? Or was he throwing away lives for no reason? How could he handle more death on his hands? No, he had to remind himself, it wasn't for him. It was for something bigger than all of them. His heart hurt, his brain ached, and his confidence wavered.

Their numbers had dwindled, but so had the Advanced Army. They'd set the eastern forest on fire, and the heat scorched him as the flames reached up into the sky. Soldiers from both sides of the battle were running frantically in all directions. The gun fire had grown chaotic when Miles heard someone yelling.

"Retreat! Retreat!"

He looked around, but it wasn't from his side. He didn't recognize the voice. Soldeirs in black uniforms ran to the south, joining their comrades, and returning to where they came from.

HABITUAL HUMANITY

Miles took a quick breath—they'd won. The Advanced Army was retreating. He couldn't believe what he was seeing.

"Are they gone?" Miles asked on the radio.

"Still retreating," Warren responded.

In disbelief, Miles walked through the woods, looking at the burned trees and dead bodies. The smell was horrific, a mixture of cedar, charcoal, and sulfur. He couldn't help it; he bent over, propped himself on his knees, and closed his eyes. Then he felt a pat on his back and stood up again, wiping his face on his sleeve. It was Ocean, covered in soot with blood running down her arm. Looking her in the eyes, he couldn't understand how relieved he was that she was okay.

"You alright?" he asked.

"Yeah. Asim says he needs you. Up the hill, he has some captives."

They emerged from the woods to see their army, those that were still alive, working hard to bury bodies or fix vehicles. Then he noticed a truck bed full of people with their hands behind their backs. He headed for it and Asim met him part of the way.

"Who do we have?" Miles asked.

"All clones. All us."

"We've got some rehabilitating to do."

"It'll take time; the orders are still strong in their mind," Asim replied. "I'll take them to base and keep them there until the orders wear off, and then see who converts. But I don't think being captives of war is going to help our case."

"Did anyone happen to come across a two-photon laser?" Miles asked. He knew it was possible, but he couldn't help but hope.

"Nope, not a single one. I haven't come across a human that wasn't on our side either. I think they implanted the orders before they left and let them at it."

Miles shook his head. Getting a laser was key to his initiative, and if he couldn't get one, how could they recruit more clones to join them? They'd have to keep recruiting more humans, more outsider communities, which meant

HABITUAL HUMANITY

more dying and losing his own.

"Head out," Miles responded and then hit the truck twice. He stepped back as the driver drove away. Miles watched the truck drive over the field, toward the road. The clones in the back stared at him with furrowed eyebrows and seeing red. It was clear they were still itching for battle.

FRIDAY | JUNE 23, 2073

GIA MORENO

It was getting to the point where there was never a normal day at work. When the clones were a secret, things were pretty predictable—stressful but predictable. Once the program became public, things got a little wild with high-profile government officials visiting, other scientists hoping to get a glimpse and asking some questions, and of course, news reporters. Once it was old news, all that went away and work returned to normal. Create an embryo, modify it, and cook it. Wash, rinse, repeat. But lately, between the war and high needs of the military and Darius losing August, nothing ever stayed the same.

Today was no different. General Maxwell entered the lab like a mountain lion protecting her cubs right in the middle of new embryos entering the tanks, which was a tedious process that required precision. It was much too easy to kill them.

"We need to talk! There's an issue with *your clones*!"

Gia's breath caught for a moment before she slowly released it and tried, without an inflection in her tone, to answer. "What's the problem?" She finished entering the code into the system and watched the robotic arm gingerly place the egg into the tank full of Mama's Recipe. She stood back once the tiny organism was inside and saw, out of the corner of her eye, Mollie and Hector leaning out of the doorway of the tech room to listen in. She tried not to make eye contact with them.

"Some of your clones have gone rogue!" the general yelled.

Gia could feel her blood pressure begin to rise. Her breath threatened to quicken. *If he knew, it wouldn't be like this.* She calmed herself by focusing on what she'd say if she wasn't guilty. With a quick jerk of her head and wide eyes she asked, "Clones have gone AWOL?"

"*Yes!* Maybe. We're not sure if their missing or AWOL, but some bases have just figured out that they have less soldiers than they're supposed to. And how can that be possible?" His voice bounced off the walls of the lab. A few interns rushed out of the room, creating a soft rustle of noise from their lab coats.

"Which clones? I can look into their history and see if there is anything that would cause a differentiation."

The general put his hands on his hips and jerked his head away from her. That gave her a huge relief, because that meant they didn't know which clones. And if they didn't know which ones, they couldn't track them to her.

"How many of them?" she asked.

He didn't change his pose; he just stood there stewing in his anger. "The President is going to have my ass," he replied in a softer tone. He turned away from her and walked around the tanks, looking up into them as though the eggs themselves were mocking him.

Gia followed him to the center of the aisle he was walking down and watched, waiting for an answer.

"They're supposed to be fool-proof. *Perfect.* The last people on earth that would turn against their country." He stopped, spun on his heel, and faced her. "If they've gone rogue, will the rest? Where did we go wrong? That's what

HABITUAL HUMANITY

I'm going to need you to find out."

"Can you give me more information on the clones that did this?" she asked, keeping her tone even. "I'll start analyzing their genome for imperfections."

Now, he kept his voice low and soft. "We're not sure which ones, to be honest. Not a single dupe hasn't reported to their post, but some bases have realized their numbers are lower than expected, ranging from fifty to a hundred dupes per base. We now know of two hundred missing soldiers, but we're checking with all bases to see if there are any others. This is probably an inside job. I can't imagine someone on the outside having that level of access." The general walked a few feet before continuing. "I want answers before I have to brief the President. I'll give you full access to the team that's looking into this, and as soon as we know which dupes, analyzing them will be your highest priority. Get a team together."

With that, the general stormed out of the lab.

Later that day, when she arrived home, Gia left her computer case in the car and rushed inside.

"Joel! Joel!" She ran through the living room, glancing briefly into the kitchen and then rushing down the hall. She found Joel in Barry's room putting together his new big boy bed.

Hearing her tone, he jumped up off the floor. "Is everything okay?"

"Some clones have gone rogue. It's only a matter of time. Where do we go, Joel? You said we'd have to stay together, but I don't know where to go or what to do." She began to hyperventilate.

"There are a few communities we can—"

"The communities the clones are attacking? We can't take Barry into a war zone! I can't have a baby in a war zone!"

Joel's face flushed in anger. "It's not like we have a choice, Gia! You made sure of that."

Gia felt all the fight go out of her. She sat down in the overstuffed brown chair next to the crib and began to cry.

HABITUAL HUMANITY

"Okay, whatever you say we need to do, I'll do it."

"We need to pack things that will be useful off the grid, both for living and for trading. And then we just need to go, get away from here. It's our only choice."

They packed up one suitcase each and took everything from pans to toys to a breast pump that they could fit in the car. Barry looked like a little doll with all the stuff piled up next to his car seat. Gia sat in the front, subconsciously touching her flat belly, terrified of giving birth off the grid. But as Joel had un-poetically pointed out, what choice did she have? They stopped by a few stores for a few more items and then drove toward the checkpoint of the community. When they pulled up, the soldier checking IDs didn't even ask for one.

"I'm sorry, you can't leave," the soldier said.

"What do you mean?" Joel asked. Gia could hear the tension in his voice.

"They've just put the communities on lock-down. The announcement is about to go out."

"Is it the war?" Joel asked.

"Not totally; the citizen scores have been frozen. We can't process anyone in or out. Any citizen that leaves cannot get back into a live-work community, so we've been directed to keep all citizens safe by keeping everyone inside."

Joel turned the car around. Neither of them spoke. They drove in silence all the way back to their home and then sat in the car in disbelief with Barry screaming in the back seat.

SATURDAY | JUNE 24, 2073

DARIUS JONES

One night during a drunken stupor, the realization hit Darius that August wasn't completely gone. How could he have not realized this before? How could he have not realized a part of August was right here on this base? August was not, in fact, gone, but a piece of him was here, right here, waiting for Darius to wise up.

Suddenly, everything lifted. He felt sober, alive. The black hole retreated until it was no more than a tiny pinpoint. The answer had been right here on the base all along.

Should he go to August now? Would that be wise? His scans would be logged and then the general might be alerted. Or would Gia be alerted? It wouldn't be so bad if Gia was alerted, but what would she say? The general, however, would be another matter entirely.

But the love of his life was waiting for him; how could he make him wait any longer? He couldn't. He'd made August wait long enough. It was his fault that August was dead, and he'd made his choices because of fear. Would he let fear keep him from August now? No, he owed him so much more than that.

He got up and got dressed for work even though it was two in the morning. He made his eggs and cleaned his dishes. Out of habit, he glanced at his watch and smiled; there was no need. He was on his own time, and the black hole was gone. Disappeared. He was free and had purpose once again. He might even throw the damn watch away. No, he wouldn't do that. He did like to know the time, after all. It was a useful device.

He stepped out of his apartment and locked the door. As soon as he emerged from the apartment building, he smiled up at the moon. Had he ever taken the time to look at the moon while he'd been here? No, the last time he'd really seen the moon was when he was in Japan with August. How fitting that he'd only just now look up at it once again.

He walked across the lawn, but he did not stop at the practice. He kept going, past the training fields that, for once, had no one in them. He walked past the administration offices and past the classroom buildings. Then, finally, the long windowless building was before him. He was supposed to have been the most excited about the lab when he received the post to work here, but, in reality, it had been the stuff of nightmares.

But not today. It wouldn't hold any nightmares today.

Darius walked straight up to the building and said, "Alaine, Darius Jones reporting for duty." What would she say? Was she smart enough to say, *It doesn't make sense to show up for duty at two in the morning, Darius Jones?*

"Hello, Darius, you may enter."

The door popped open just like it was a normal time of day. Just like he was supposed to report for duty. Just like it was bright daylight and August was alive again. *It is meant to be.*

He walked inside the quiet lab. He peered up at all the tiny embryos floating in the gigantic tubes. It was perfect timing, since Gia had created these just yesterday.

He veered right and entered the monitoring room and

without hesitation scanned his ID card. The clear glass computer screens in front of him came to life, showing him the statistics of the cells floating within the tubes in the adjacent room. But he didn't care about them. He then laughed out loud at that thought; no truer statement had ever been uttered inside of him. He honestly didn't give a damn about those clones! He hated them. No, he despised them!

"Pull up soldier records."

The screens immediately switched and pulled up a data base. At first he thought, *How strange*. But it wasn't, not really. The only person who had higher credentials than him was Gia. And he was assigned to assist her in all matters relating to the project. For her to be successful, she had to have the DNA of all the soldiers that had come before them. She used the best DNA, as determined by the military anyway, to create the perfect soldiers. None of them had known when they'd signed up that they'd given the military permission to use their DNA in any way it saw fit. They'd all thought they were having their genome profiled as a means of identification, or for health purposes, particularly if they were injured during their service. But no, it was for creation and manipulation. Had August been cloned already? Was there another August?

He knew Gia better than that. Even if his DNA had been included at any given time, she'd never only use a single strand. There was too much risk in such a move. No, every clone out there had been carefully modified to be a melting pot, so to speak, of DNA. A little of this, a little of that. And he had the same access to these records as she did because he was the only one that could come close to recreating her work.

But he couldn't. He had no idea where to start. He was not a geneticist, he was an endocrinologist. Those were vastly different practices. As much as he'd learned from her (and oh, he had learned), he'd never completely created a clone before.

But that's not what he was doing, was it? He wasn't

creating one of their clones. He was creating a person. A genuine, true person.

It wouldn't be right to make another August, to hide him and force him to live in confusion. Besides, it wouldn't be August. It would be a young copy, and not the man he loved but one that couldn't possibly hold the same experiences and feelings. That's not what he was doing here today. He wasn't going to hurt his partner more than he already had.

"August Paxton."

The records popped up.

"Darius Jones."

His own records popped up. It wasn't the first time he looked at himself from an unfeeling perspective. All members of the team had grown curious enough to look up their own genetic profile to see how well they lined up and how useful they truly were to the military. It was unfortunate they could do this because the results never mirrored their own perspectives. Each individual knows all the experiences, creativity, family, love, and more that make them who they are, but to look at one's own profile and see that you've been determined as "emotionally distant" as Darius saw on his profile, which made him desirable as a clone but not as an employee, was a strange experience. He'd seen it before, and *Fuck them*, he thought. He didn't care about how he was analyzed at this time. Right now, he wanted purity.

"Merge DNA profiles."

The computer immediately offered multiple possible outcomes of not only body types and facial features, but also personalities. He hadn't anticipated picking and choosing what would be a part of their child. He'd wanted it to be involuntary, chance. He wanted it to be a pure experience. A true moment of love, of passion bringing two people together, and then a surprising, glorious creation from their love. How could he begin to choose what parts of them were to be included or, worse, excluded? Weren't they supposed to love each other for better or for worse, to love all aspects and sides, no matter how negative? Would choosing to purposefully not include something now be the same as saying there was a part of August he didn't love?

He couldn't face that.

He tried to think of an aspect that could be easily used and chosen out of love. Health. Which of these possibilities would provide the healthiest child? Isn't that all August would want? Below each outcome were percentages of mental capabilities, life span, and health problems. He'd choose the best outcome from his selections. Strong mind, meaning no black holes, longest possible life span, and no health problems that would be too detrimental to live a good life. Then came the big question: boy or girl? What would August have wanted? But it wasn't about August anymore, it was about honoring August, and that would mean choosing the one that best suited Darius, as Darius would have to care for the child. That would be a boy, because Darius didn't know the first thing about girls.

"Create."

He walked over to the biological 3-D printer. It turned and moved, like a mother bird making a nest. This bird would only take thirty minutes to pop out an embryo.

Once the embryo was complete, Darius slid on the special gloves and took the round, oddly fleshy and sticky organism into the warehouse. It didn't seem right to leave something so important alone in metal unfeeling tanks, but he had no other option. He didn't have to let robotic arms place it in the tank though, he could at least carry it to it's temporary home. With shaking hands he walked to the next available tank, which was already filled with Mama's Recipe and waiting for its occupant. He gingerly placed the embryo inside. He could feel his heart pounding in his chest, ready to go to war for this little being.

With the tank closed, he turned his attention to the control panel. He didn't want this child to be a man when he emerged. He also couldn't handle a newborn by himself and keep it secret. In the control panel, he punched *6 0 Enter*. He'd have a five-year-old in sixty days.

SATURDAY | JUNE 24, 2073

MILES

In the large colorless mess hall, Miles sat alone at a long empty table. He'd missed dinner and almost missed eating entirely, for they were already cleaning up the kitchen. The smell of bleach burned his nose while the smell of lemon chicken made his stomach rumble.

Aside from the smell of cleaner, Miles didn't mind eating alone from time to time. As the one with the vision, he always had people approaching him, asking questions, and wondering what they were to do now. They'd ask everything from who was to have the porta potties cleaned out to war strategy.

The worst were the problems that didn't have solutions. It wasn't their fault—the problem was numbers. They needed more clones and more humans to fight with them in order to have a chance. The more people, the more beds, food, weapons, and clothes were needed. It was an interesting situation to be in; he was constantly problem-solving, and that repetition made it something he was good at. The whole leadership idea was kind of funny, as it meant continually being in a corner and finding a way out.

HABITUAL HUMANITY

While he sat there pondering the numbers, she walked in, the woman with thick, long brown hair. She had a short and tiny body, but with a hint of firecracker somewhere inside of her. He wondered if she also sought the solitude of a dinner long over like he did.

When she walked in, he almost choked on his green beans, but thankfully she didn't see him. He wasn't sure what she would do if she did, as many times as she'd caught him staring at her. She probably assumed he thought of her romantically. He was sure plenty of men and women had tried to gain her attention.

After she got her food from the line, he seized the chance. He slowly extended his long arm into a huge, unmistakable wave and then gestured to the seat across from him with an open hand. She looked behind her as though he couldn't possibly have been motioning to her. Then she looked down at her food, over at him, and with her head down, began to walk in his direction. He couldn't believe that she walked with her head down. Mother would never walk with such little confidence. But yet, every part of this woman was every bit his mother, he had no doubt.

"Hi, I'm Miles," he said when she was close enough.

"I know who you are," she replied.

Good, she does have Mother's fire. "But I need to know *you*."

"Gianna." She looked him in the eye for a brief second as she said it.

"Join me."

She eyed him before she sat down.

"Found any interesting material in those books you read?" Miles asked.

Her eyes shot directly at his once again. "How do you know about my books?"

"I keep up with you." He shoved a forkful of chicken in his mouth trying to seem casual and not like the weirdo that stared at her all the time. "So, what are they about?"

Her flesh turned a bright red. "I just like to read."

"Let me see, if I were a guessing person, I'd say you're

reading about genetics."

Her eyes went wide, and she put down her fork that held a steamed baby carrot.

"Don't look so alarmed," Miles laughed.

"How could you know that?" she demanded.

Miles lowered his voice and leaned over his plate of food. "There are a few of us that aren't like the others. There are a few of us that were *designed* to be different, to be leaders. Ten of us. But I'd only found nine of us, that is until I saw you. I've been searching for you for quite some time."

"Designed to be different? That doesn't add up."

"No?"

"What is it that makes you think you're special? And why, by just looking at me, would you know I'm the missing one?"

"Because I met the woman who designed us. She's a purposeful woman, and certainly not one to create four females and five males."

Now, Gianna no longer avoided eye contact. She looked at him as though he was unbelievable, like he was a ghost. "And why do you think *I'm* the missing one?"

"Because you are her. You are *her* clone."

Gianna's eyes grew wide as though something in her clicked. Her eyes shifted quickly.

"You knew that you're her clone?" he asked, not afraid to reveal he saw her brief expression.

"No, I didn't."

"Then there's something you *do* know."

"No, there's not." She got up, abandoning her tray of uneaten food, and walked out.

TUESDAY | JUNE 27, 2073

STELLA HOPKINS

The heartache was so deep it felt like it left an actual bruise on her entire body. It hurt to be awake. It hurt to speak. It hurt to be touched, even to breathe. How could she exist without him?

But you need to be there for Jevan. It was Deon's voice in her mind, telling her the truth.

I know, but I need time, she replied.

He needs you now, Deon said in his serious voice.

He's strong.

Not as strong as he seems. He needs you.

She sat up in their bed and stared at the wall, waiting for the pain to subside. But it didn't. It just kept eating away at her heart. She got up anyway and walked down the hall to Jevan's room. He was playing video games with Sean. *Thank God for Sean.* But then Stella remembered the painful truth that her best friend was gone too, and the pain was anew. She had to adjust her thoughts. *Thank God they have each other.*

"Hey, hun!" Stella said through the cracked door.

"Mom! You're up! Would you like some tea?" Jevan

asked. Sean glanced back and forth between them as though not sure what to say. Stella understood, because Sean was hurting too. They were all hurting.

"I was going to ask if you two would like some cookies," Stella said.

"Like, fresh cookies?" Jevan asked.

"Is there any other kind?" Stella tried to sound normal, but her voice cracked.

"What kind?" Sean asked, his voice as soft as the day he came to this community. He'd gotten stronger and braver over the years, but now, in the aftermath of his mother's death, his vulnerable side had returned. Stella vowed it'd only be for a time and that she'd help him, just as Naomi would have helped Jevan.

"Well, oatmeal raisin." None of them had seen chocolate in years, but it's funny what the lack of something like chocolate will do, even to a kid. It was the only thing Jevan would eat before, but now oatmeal raisin would just have to be the number one cookie.

"Yay! Cookies!" Jevan said, looking over at Sean. He seemed to give him the *be positive* look.

"Yeah!" Sean offered.

Stella walked into the kitchen only to stop short because Miles, Ocean, and Jake were sitting at her table. She was still sure she'd never get used to that freaky eye the clones had. Maybe she could find a way to eradicate it.

"What's going on?" Stella asked, pulling down the oats from her pantry.

"I'm just talking to Jake here about next steps," Miles said.

Stella couldn't help it; she involuntarily barked a grim laugh. "Next steps? We just buried our spouses a few days ago, Miles. Maybe your kind doesn't know the pain that entails."

Jake got up and limped across the room, putting his hand on Stella's shoulder and squeezing it. He'd never done anything like that before, but he was doing these small

HABITUAL HUMANITY

gestures a lot. Naomi had always had his back. Deon had always had Stella's. Now, they attempted to have each other's backs, but it was awkward and didn't feel natural. Does anyone know what to do in times like these?

"It's too early to talk about such things, Jake."

"As far as we know, they're still making more soldiers, so more soldiers will come for us. I know it's too soon, but we don't want our sons to grow up like this, preparing for war right after finishing one. We need to fight for peace so that they can know peace," Jake said.

"We need to take down Fort Campbell. If we can stop them from making more soldiers, we'll have a chance," Miles added.

"We can't hide forever. And the time to strike back is now," Ocean said.

Stella turned and threw the container of oats across the room, smashing it against the wall, sending the small white flakes flying everywhere like confetti. She began to sob. Even when she heard the footsteps of Jevan and Sean running down the hall, she couldn't stop crying. Jake had grabbed her shoulders to comfort her, but when Jevan entered the room, Jake moved to the side. Jevan hugged his mom and she hugged him back.

"What is it, Mom?"

"They want to keep fighting, Jevan. I can't fight anymore. I thought I could, but I can't."

"You don't have to," he replied.

"What?" Stella pushed him away just far enough to look into his eyes.

"You're not a fighter, you're a healer. But the fighters should keep fighting. It's the only way."

ACKNOWLEDGEMENTS

Allies exists because of a supportive and loving group of people I like to refer to as Team 2020. I'm so grateful to Brad Tompkins, Meg M. Robinson, Justin Joseph, Jennifer Drummand, Kitty Wynn Gavel, Elaine Tompkins, Darcy Werkman (AKA The Bearded Book Editor), RebecaCovers, Chris Negron, and Toni Bellon. And to both of my writing groups, you are the first eyes on every project. Thank you.

ABOUT THE AUTHOR

J. M. Tompkins was born in Atlanta and grew up in a small Georgia town. She studied at Emory University and has worked as a flight attendant and within technology sales. Determined to make her life's goals come true, she started her own publishing company and began focusing on her true passions.

As an author, she first published at the age of sixteen, has had a popular poetry blog, published in several magazines, and began working on what would become the Habitual Humanity Series in 2012. She finally took the plunge in 2019 to begin publishing her books.

J. M.'s writings combine several of her passions including people, nature, science, and technology. Within her writing, she loves to explore what she refers to as interesting science with her fears of what our future society might be like. Interesting science, according to J. M., is the science of today that a large portion of the population still thinks of as science fiction. This includes the possibilities of what can be achieved with Artificial Intelligence, personal data, biohacking, genetic modifications, and more.

J. M currently lives in Georgia and enjoys camping and hiking with her husband, son, and dogs.

Made in the USA
Columbia, SC
05 March 2022